What'll We Do With

WEIRD UNCLE WILL?

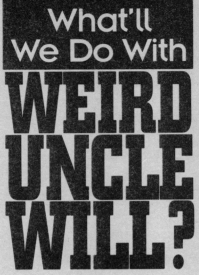

What'll We Do With
WEIRD UNCLE WILL?

VeraLee Wiggins

R

REVIEW AND HERALD® PUBLISHING ASSOCIATION
HAGERSTOWN, MD 21740

This book was
Edited by Gerald Wheeler
Designed by Bill Kirstein
Cover art by John Buxton
Typeset: 10/11 Schoolbook

PRINTED IN U.S.A.

98 97 96 95 94 93   10 9 8 7 6 5 4 3 2 1

Library of Congress Cataloging in Publication Data

Wiggins, VeraLee, 1928-
      What'll we do with weird Uncle Will / VeraLee Wiggins.
         p.   cm.
      I. Title.
      PS3573.I386W47   1993
      813' .54—dc20

ISBN 0-8280-0695-4

Dedication:

For Leroy, my dearest love
for longer than I care to remember.
The one who's always there for me,
always helping, always encouraging.
Who loves me when I no longer love myself.
Thank you, Sweetie Pie.
I'll love you forever and ever.

CHAPTER

1

Responding to his mother's summons, Dirk Ward dropped heavily onto the couch beside her. "I thought Ron would never leave," she said, patting his knee.

"Why'd you want him to leave?" Dirk asked. Ron Reed had been his closest friend forever—at least as long as he could remember—and spent plenty of time hanging around the Ward house.

Evidently hearing his family talking, Dad wandered in from the den, his home office. "Let's have worship," he said. "Then we need to talk to you." The Ward family enjoyed reading some verses from the Bible each night, then praying together. That evening Dirk thought that his father emphasized "help us to do Your will" a little more than usual during his prayer. Something must be up.

After they all prayed, Mr. Ward sat on the couch beside Mom and took her hand in his, caressing it gently. Dad seemed nervous, and now that Dirk thought about it, Mom did too. *This must be serious*. Dirk moved to the rocker so he could see them both, but their expressions were unreadable. While they didn't look angry, neither did they appear all that happy. "What did I do?" he asked, smoothing down his second cowlick, the one that always stuck straight up.

Grinning, Mom reached her free hand over and messed up his thick dark brown hair. "Do we talk to you only when you do something wrong?"

With a shrug he shoved his hair down again.

"No, son," Dad said, "it isn't what you did. It's what we're all going to do." He hesitated, then plunged ahead. "We're about to have a new family member, and I hope it'll be nice for you. Uncle Will is coming to live with us."

Dirk jumped completely off the seat of the rocker. "No," he said, shaking his dark head. "I like Uncle Will all right, but he can't live with us."

"Why not?" Mom asked. "And where's he going to live?"

Dropping back to the chair, Dirk rocked furiously for a moment before answering. He glanced from one parent to the other, seeking reassurance, finding none. "You know," he said softly. "He's— funny."

Although Dad frowned, Mom managed a smile. "He's just a little mixed up sometimes," she said. "Most of the time he's fine, and you'd look a long time to find a more refined old gentleman. And the thing is, if we don't take him, he'll have to go to a nursing home."

"So let him." Dirk felt a little ashamed of his remark as soon as it cleared his lips, but he didn't retract it.

"Come on, Dirk," Mom said quietly. "Don't be a jerk."

Dad released Mom's hand, clasped his own together, and steepled his fingers. Then he looked directly into Dirk's eyes. "Do you remember the Bible verse, 'Inasmuch as you've done it to the least of these?' That means if we do something for someone who needs help, it's the same as doing it for

Jesus." He watched Dirk another moment. "Well," he added, his voice gruff, "Uncle Will's not going to any nursing home until he has to. He feels strongly about that, and so do I. I doubt he'll be any trouble anyway. He just needs a place where he can be sure to get good meals and a little care." Meeting Dirk's eyes once more, he nodded, then gave Mom's hand a squeeze and kissed her. "I have a little more work to do, Rosa," he said. Getting to his feet, he vanished into his den-office.

"You two already decided, didn't you?" Dirk asked Mom.

With a nod she pulled him close for a couple of seconds, giving his shoulders a little squeeze. "We had no choice. The doctors say he's not competent to live alone anymore, but far from needing to be in a nursing home." She watched Dirk a moment before continuing. "I'm sure you won't mind having your uncle here after you get used to the idea."

"He's not *my* uncle," Dirk insisted. "And if he comes, I'll never have my friends over again. I'll be too embarrassed. Let him go live with Grandpa and Grandma. They don't have any kids to embarrass. Anyway, he's more their age." Uncle Will was really Dad's uncle, Grandpa's older brother. That made him Dirk's great-uncle.

Mom shook her own dark head. "They offered to take him, but we couldn't let them. This is their time to enjoy each other. If they lived around here, he could live with them, and we could help out. But the way things are, we're it. Now you try to forget all about this for a few days. By then you'll be used to the idea."

Dirk sat and thought a moment, then decided that he'd never be used to the idea. There had to be a way to stop it, even though he couldn't think of it at the moment. He'd work on it. But for now he might as well stay calm. As he headed toward the hallway, he said over his shoulder, "At least we have plenty of bedrooms." Besides his and his parents' rooms, they had two guest rooms upstairs, as well as a small sitting room and two baths.

"Dad's moving the office upstairs so Uncle Will can have the den for his bedroom," Mom replied. "He gets around pretty well, but since he'll be alone all day, the doctor said he shouldn't be climbing up and down the stairs. He could fall, you know. After all, 87 is getting right up there."

Because the den had been Dad's private office ever since he could remember, Dirk could hardly believe his ears. His father had allowed him in it only the last few years. "When's Uncle Will coming?" he asked, fearing the answer.

"Dad's taking a day off work next week to move him in. Probably Monday. I hope you'll make him feel welcome. He's even less eager to live here than you are to have him." She waited a moment, then added, "Think of this, Dirk. At his age, he isn't going to be with us forever."

Dirk raided the refrigerator for an orange, then ran up the carpeted stairs to his bedroom. Dropping into the chair at his desk, he opened his algebra book. After staring at the page a few minutes he discovered he couldn't concentrate. Slamming the covers together, he shoved the book into a drawer. He had enough trouble with algebra when his mind wasn't spinning. Peeling the orange, he dropped the rinds into his wastebasket.

Maybe Uncle Will wouldn't be with them forever, but it sounded that way to Dirk. It could be five years. By then he'd be almost 20, halfway through college. When he reached for another section of orange, he found the fruit was gone. He didn't remember eating it.

Crawling between the sheets, he wondered how crazy Uncle Will really was. He'd seen the old man several times when they'd visited Grandpa and Grandma. Since he'd heard about Uncle Will's "eccentricities" as Dad called his condition, Dirk had especially watched his great-uncle but had seen only small memory lapses. Nothing big. But he knew Dad would never say anything about his favorite uncle if it weren't true.

Well, if Uncle Will came, Dirk would just become a hermit. His friends would have to find someplace else to gather. He couldn't imagine living without friends, but he wasn't about to set himself up to be embarrassed every time he turned around. No way. "Dear Father," he whispered, "please don't let it happen. Don't let that old man come here and ruin my life."

Though he didn't tell a soul about the impending calamity, it didn't leave his mind for many hours at a time.

The following Monday Dirk couldn't decide whether he felt relief that the waiting was over, or if he'd simply accepted that his life was finished.

Anyway, when he arrived home from basketball practice, he found Uncle Will in the living room, sitting as straight as if he were a much younger individual. The man wore an immaculate light gray suit, snowy white shirt, and black tie—and busied himself reading the newspaper.

"Hi, Uncle Will," Dirk called as he passed through. "Welcome to our family."

The stately old man folded the paper neatly in his lap. "Hello there, John. Come, sit down, and we'll have a good visit."

John? His father was John. How could Uncle Will think he was his father? Dad had blond hair, and Dirk's was almost as dark as Mom's. And he hoped he didn't look quite as old as Dad. Dirk sat in the rocker. "I'm Dirk. Did you get all settled?"

"I know who you are," Uncle Will said, looking

as if he were using every ounce of his patience. "Yes, I guess I'm settled. They put my things in that room down the hall. I wanted to be upstairs but I understand that part of the house is restricted to family."

The old man looked so forlorn that Dirk felt sorry for him in spite of himself. "You're family, Uncle Will," he said. "Dad put you in the den because the doctor was afraid you'd fall down the stairs."

They talked a few more minutes, then Mom called them for supper.

Uncle Will stood, straight and steady. "Come on," he said, "we can wash up together."

Dirk swished his hands under the water and reached for the towel but Uncle Will stopped him. "Hey!" the old man said, "don't you know what soap's for?" He pumped a tablespoon of liquid soap over his own palm, then another into Dirk's. Dirk scrubbed his hands thoroughly. At least he wasn't going to have to worry about Uncle Will being a dirty old man.

Uncle Will's table manners were impeccable, and occasionally he corrected Dirk's lapses. After supper the boy raced up the stairs to do his home work. Resting his chin in his hand, he did some serious thinking. His great-uncle had seemed in complete control all evening except for calling him John once. And anyone could call a person by the wrong name once in a while.

After he finished his homework, the family had worship together. Uncle Will read his Bible verses flawlessly, and prayed as sensibly and sincerely as anyone Dirk had ever heard. But he ended his prayer by asking the Lord to help people realize he was perfectly capable of caring for himself.

Then they watched a rerun of "The Newhart Show." "That's an inane program," Uncle Will said when it ended. "Imagine two brothers with the same name." His saggy old face brightened. "At least they didn't all kill each other as they do in most shows these days."

"After you get to know the characters, it's pretty cute, Uncle Will," Mom said. "Do you have any special programs you'd like to watch? Be sure to tell us if you do." She giggled. "That is, if they don't kill each other."

"Uncle Will doesn't watch that kind of thing, Rosa," Dad said. Turning to Mom sitting beside him, he pulled her closer and kissed her lightly on the lips. Uncle Will looked embarrassed and glanced away.

Dirk chuckled to himself. *The old guy better start getting used to that. Mom and Dad have always acted as if they've just gotten married.* Dirk didn't mind. In fact, he kind of liked it.

By that time the next program came on and everyone fell silent. Mom, Dad, and Dirk hardly ever watched TV so Dirk knew they felt nervous about Uncle Will too, and didn't know how to entertain him. About halfway through the program the elderly man excused himself and said he was going to bed. When that program ended, Dirk ate a pink-cheeked Granny Smith apple with a glass of milk and hit the stairs. He felt more than ready for bed too.

When he flipped on his light, he gasped in surprise. Uncle Will lay in his bed! The wrinkled face lay turned to the wall, the covers tucked snugly under the sagging chin.

2

Dirk couldn't believe how soundly Uncle Will slept. He didn't even react when the bright light hit his face.

"Hey!" the boy yelled. "What are you doing in my bed?"

Uncle Will jerked to his other side and sat up, blinking as if wondering where he was. Mom rushed in just before Dad stuck his head into the room. "What's all the racket about?" Mr. Ward asked.

Silently Dirk pointed at his bed with Uncle Will sitting in it, still looking dazed.

Dad helped Uncle Will up, wrapped his plush maroon robe around his shoulders, and led him down the stairs.

"Where are some clean sheets?" Dirk asked when the two men disappeared.

Mom went after the bed clothing. "Uncle Will is really clean," she said gently as she helped Dirk put on the fresh linen.

"I know. But I don't want him in my bed. I don't want anyone in my bed." Dirk didn't mean that exactly as he said it. What he really didn't want was the old wrinkled man in his bed. When Dirk finally crawled between the clean, fresh-smelling sheets he renewed his determination not to have anyone over again—ever. The Sabbath school youth class had lots of parties at Dirk's house. But no more.

The next evening Dirk completed a trade he'd been working on for some time. He boxed up the electric train set he'd had since his ninth birthday, and Dad drove him to the other side of the little town of Pine Crest to Jack McHann's.

"You sure you've thought this over?" Dad asked for the tenth time when they stopped at the McHann place. "We've had a lot of fun with that train."

Dirk nodded once more. "We used to, but how long's it been since we set it up?"

Dad shrugged and opened his door. "OK, let's go." He pulled the key from the ignition.

Jack, looking excited, came to the door and reached for the big train box.

He put it on something just inside the house, then stepped onto the porch. "I'll help you get the go-cart," he said, leading the way around the house.

Dirk felt himself swell with pride when he saw the rusty-green low-to-the-ground machine. He couldn't wait to get it running.

"Have you checked that thing out?" Dad asked, sounding not at all impressed.

"Yeah," Dirk replied. "I've been looking it over for quite a while. It's a mean machine."

Dad shrugged. "Could have fooled me." But he helped the boys load it into the back of the pickup. "Does it run?" Dad asked on the way home.

Dirk shook his head. "Not yet, but just wait. I'll have it going in nothing flat."

"Where you going to drive it?"

"I'll think of something. Maybe I can make a track on the place somewhere."

Uncle Will found the right bed that night, so Dirk figured at least one problem had been solved.

Ron Reed, who lived across the street from the Wards, and Dirk both played on the basketball team, so they stayed late at school several nights each week for practice. The team captain and best player by far, Ron was six feet and stood three inches taller than Dirk. He specialized in three-point shots. In fact, he seemed unable to miss the basket at any distance. Practice, which Dirk usually enjoyed, seemed to last forever the next day. He couldn't wait to show Ron his go-cart. Not only would Ron be excited, but he knew a little bit about making them run.

Finally the boys rode their bikes into Dirk's yard. He opened the garage door and proudly led Ron to the back corner where Dad had helped him park it. "What do you think?" he asked.

Ron checked the cart over carefully before he answered. "We can get it going," he finally said, straightening up. "It'll just take a little time and some money."

Time was scarce, but they'd find it somewhere. But money. That was the one thing Dirk didn't happen to have at the moment. Whenever he got hold of any, it seemed to disappear like smoke.

As the boys checked different parts of the little machine, Dirk heard the back door of the house open. A moment later Uncle Will stood beside them. "What do you call that thing?" he asked.

Oh, brother. Dirk hadn't wanted his friends to ever hear about his great uncle, let alone see him. He'd counted on the old man staying in the house at least until the weather warmed up. But here he was, already intruding. "It's a go-cart," Dirk answered, unable to be rude. "What do you think of it?"

"I don't know," Uncle Will said, looking completely serious. "I'll have to see it running and ride in it before I can tell. Think we could crank it up today?"

Ron let out one of his cackling laughs. "Good for you," he said loudly, "but you'll have to wait a few days until we figure out how to get it going."

Uncle Will nodded. "I guess I can do that." He turned and walked to the house, his shoulders back and his chin high.

"Who's that old dude?" Ron asked.

Dirk didn't want to tell him one thing about Uncle Will, but he couldn't think of any way out. "He's my great-uncle. He moved in with us yesterday but I don't want anyone to know. His book's missing some important pages, if you know what I mean."

Ron's eyes widened, then he grinned. "He seemed all right to me. Looked like a banker or something."

"He used to be an attorney, then a judge. That was all before his lights dimmed."

As they talked, Mom drove into the driveway. "Hi, guys," she called, hurrying to the back door.

Ron soon took off across the road. After one last look at his go-cart, Dirk pushed it back into the corner, lowered the garage door, and followed Mom into the house.

"Who left the back door open?" she asked the second he set foot inside.

"Uncle Will came out for a few minutes."

Mom didn't look too pleased. "He let out about five dollar's worth of heat. You'll have to watch him."

Since Dirk hadn't gotten home much earlier then his mother, and Uncle Will hadn't come outside until then, Dirk wondered how the old man could have possibly wasted so much heat. But he didn't ask.

That night after the family prayed together, Uncle Will called Dirk to him. "That boy you had in the garage today," he began, "did you know he's Negro?"

For a fraction of a second Dirk wondered if the

old man had short-circuited again. Then it hit him. "Oh, you mean Ron. Yeah, I guess he's Black. I never think about it."

"Do you think you should associate with him?"

"Why wouldn't I? He's my best friend."

"Are you aware that the people with whom you associate alter your reputation?"

Dirk didn't like the trend of the conversation so he got up to go. "I hope so. He's a great guy. I'm lucky he hangs out with me." He ran up the stairs to his bedroom to study.

As he attacked his Spanish assignment, his mind went over the confrontation with his uncle. He'd just encountered racism for the first time in his life, and he didn't like it. The Reeds had lived across the road for as long as Dirk could remember. Both families belonged to the little Pine Crest Seventh-day Adventist Church. Since the small town had no church school, the boys had always gone to public school together. Once in a while skin color had come up in their conversation, but it had been natural, with no suggestion of one being better than the other.

The next morning Dirk told his mother what Uncle Will had said. "I'll have to keep them apart," he added. "I'd feel awful if he said something to Ron."

Mom shook her long dark hair. "He won't. He's a perfect gentleman. In fact, he'll probably never mention it to you again, either. Really, Dirk, he meant well."

The next morning Dirk noticed a new girl in freshman English. Just looking at her made him forget where he was and what he was supposed to be doing. He'd never seen hair exactly that color, light blonde with the faintest streaks of red. Her cheeks looked like peaches against flawless ivory skin. And her eyes! The color of spring grass—and sparkling as if she'd just heard a fantastic joke. All in a tiny, slim girl.

The teacher asked the class to hand in their homework, and for a second Dirk didn't remember whether he'd done it.

As the kids hurried to science, Jack McHann slapped Dirk on the back. "I never saw anyone so out of it, Ward," he said. "Admit it, you were in a daze. And all because of the new girl."

"Well, what did *you* think?" Dirk demanded.

The round-faced boy hesitated only a moment. "Not too bad."

The Spanish teacher finally introduced the new girl. Celia Gould. Dirk had never heard such a beautiful name in his life. Celia. Somehow he felt as if it would be wonderful to say it over and over all day long. He thought he couldn't bear it when he had to leave her to go to P.E.

That night Dirk tried to push Celia from his mind long enough to figure out what he'd need to get his go-cart going. With Ron's help he decided it would take about $20, which he still didn't have.

He could shovel snow to earn money, but March was really too late for that and too early for lawn mowing. Besides, they didn't have any close neighbors except the Reeds. And Ron always had their place shoveled or mowed long before Dirk got around to doing his.

"I need some money to get my go-cart running," Dirk announced after worship that night. "How could I earn some?"

Uncle Will brightened up. "There are lots of ways to earn money," he said. "How about a paper route? I'll help you."

Dirk shook his head. "Three kids already have the area, and they've been doing it for five years. I guess they plan to continue forever."

"Box boy?"

Dirk shook his head. "I have basketball practice."

Uncle Will made a few more suggestions but someone had a reason why each wouldn't work.

Later when Dirk started to slide into his bed he found a $50 bill lying on his pillow. *How did that get there?* But he knew almost before he wondered. Uncle Will had left it there so he could go ahead and fix up the go-cart. *Hey, maybe it wouldn't be so bad having the old man around after all.* But he couldn't accept it! Throwing on his blue robe, he ran downstairs and showed the big bill to his parents. He thrust it at his father. "Here, you give it back to him."

His eyes softening, Dad shook his head. "He wants you to have it. This reminds me of when I was a boy. Uncle Will slipped me more money than you can imagine. Anytime he heard I needed something, he gave me the exact amount. And he took me on lots of vacations: Disneyland, Yellowstone National Park, Vancouver Island. But you know the best thing he ever did for me? Uncle Will and Aunt Esther were the ones who first became Christians. He gently and lovingly taught Mom, Dad, and me about Jesus' great love and sacrifice for us. The man's done more for me than I'll ever do for him, Dirk."

Dirk swallowed. He'd known Dad loved Uncle Will a lot, but he hadn't heard all of that stuff. For a second he wished he had an uncle like that. Then he remembered he did, only to instantly correct himself again. The man living with them wasn't the same person who'd been so good to Dad. Finally he thought of the money again. "Are you saying I should keep it?" he asked.

"I'm not sure. That's a lot of money for a kid. And it could become a habit." He hesitated as though thinking hard. "Then again," he finally continued, "Uncle Will doesn't have much to spend his money on anymore."

Dirk stared at the $50 bill. It would enable him to fix the go-cart and have money left over. "I know," he said. "I'll return it when I get the money."

Dad's face brightened. "Sounds good. And I'll make sure you're able to earn the money to pay him back. You can work during your spring break if you don't have a chance before."

Taking the bill, Dirk raced back upstairs. He'd helped Dad a couple of summers now and had enjoyed it. An electrical contractor, Dad let him assist some of his employees in simple things like running after tools or whatever the men needed. Sometimes he drilled holes in studs, the two-by-fours that divided the rooms, for the electrical wiring to run through.

The next day Dirk hurried to English, his first class, eager to see Celia. When he spotted her, her smile almost overwhelmed him, even though it wasn't directed at him. Although he didn't approach her or try to talk to her, he enjoyed being in the same room with her.

When school ended that day, he found a surprise at basketball practice. Another new student. Pine Crest High hardly ever had new kids but this one made two within a week! A blonde girl, about five feet nine, almost his exact height, dribbled the ball beneath the basket. She sank one basket after another. Dirk watched her step back and sink one from 20 feet. He couldn't believe his eyes when she made two more long shots. Too bad she wasn't a guy. With her height and sharp eye, she'd be hard to stop. Another reason she should have been a guy—she wasn't pretty. Her blonde hair looked soft enough and her large bright-blue eyes seemed intelligent and expressive, but she just didn't have it for a girl.

The coach blew his whistle to call the boys to the center of the floor. "This is Donna Kind," he said, sounding cranky. "She's trying out for the team."

"But she's a girl," a dozen boys protested at the same time, each in his own words.

"I think we can all see that," Mr. Brimley, the coach, growled. "She says she has the right to play on the school team if she's qualified, so that's what we have to find out."

They divided the players, and Brimley tossed the ball for the tip-off. Donna didn't happen to be on the same side as Dirk, but he watched closely to see how she played.

It bothered him when the players tried harder to keep the ball from her than they did the opposing team. The three times she managed to secure the ball she scored, but with the lack of teamwork her side lost the game, 19-33.

The young people gathered around Brimley again when he blew his whistle. "That's all for today," he snapped.

"What about the girl?" someone yelled.

Dirk could feel the coach's indecision before he answered. He thought he knew what the man was thinking. Did the girl have a fair chance? Did they really have to let her play with the boys? "We'll talk about it tomorrow," the tall man said, then walked off. Usually he spent time with his boys before leaving.

"What did you think of the girl?" Dirk asked Ron as they rode their bikes home.

His friend grinned. "She's plenty good," he said with enthusiasm, "and you know it."

Dirk pedaled a few minutes, thinking. Ron was right, and every boy there had recognized that fact. Finally he met Ron's eyes. "Yeah, but why can't she play on the girls' team?"

Ron started to answer, then stopped to spit out a bug that had flown into his mouth. "What kind of girls' team does Pine Crest High have?" he asked a moment later. "It wouldn't be even a challenge to her. And I'm not sure the girls have a team at all."

After that they talked about other things but Dirk kept thinking about Donna, the basketball-playing amazon.

When he reached home he ran into his bathroom upstairs and found seven towels hanging over the shower curtain bar. Touching them, he discovered they were all damp. What had Uncle Will been doing? He wasn't even supposed to be upstairs, let alone using Dirk's bathroom.

"I took a shower," Uncle Will explained when he asked him.

"But why seven towels?"

"Did I use seven towels?" Uncle shook his head. "No, those towels were already there when I showered. I took them down so I wouldn't get water on the floor and hung them back up when I finished."

Dirk told his parents about it after the old man had gone to bed. Dad took Mom's hand and held it tight. He and Mom looked at each other and giggled. "That's easy," Dad said. "He took seven showers."

Dirk sat silently, too shocked to answer.

"He always takes lots of showers," Mom said, "but he usually does it downstairs in his own bathroom. He may have taken a few in his own bathroom today too."

Neither Mom nor Dad seemed upset. In fact, both chuckled again. "Why is it funny?" Dirk asked. "And what about all the times you've yelled at me for wasting water with long showers?"

Mom squeezed Dad's hand and dropped it, then gave Dirk a hug, releasing him before he could object. "Honey," she said, "you know how fussy I am about keeping things clean. My big worry when Uncle Will came was that he'd be a pig. I'd much rather he'd take a dozen showers a day, which he has on at least two different occasions, than to wonder if he'd had one in the last week. And as for the hot water, he pays room and board, you know. Much more than it costs to keep him."

Dirk shook his head. "No, I didn't know."

"He wouldn't have it any other way," Dad explained. "Anyway, I guess it's his privilege to take as many showers as he likes. But maybe we can get him to stick to his own bathroom."

Dirk and Ron got the go-cart almost ready to run that afternoon. Uncle Will didn't appear while they worked on the machine.

The following Saturday night after worship, Uncle Will asked what time everyone went to bed on weekends.

Mom shrugged. "We go to bed when we can't hold our eyes open any longer. Why?"

The elderly man grinned sort of sheepishly. "Well, you told me to let you know if I wanted to watch any special programs. I do have one that I always enjoy. It's "The World's Best Wrestling," and it comes on at midnight. Think anyone would mind if I watched it?"

Three heads shook from side to side. "We don't mind," Dad finally said, "but I can't believe you like that stuff."

The old man chuckled happily. "It's my favorite sport, but it does get a little rough sometimes. Why don't you watch it with me?"

"Sure," Mom said, giggling.

Dad put his arms around her and pulled her close. "If Rosa watches, I'll have to watch too. I can't have my best girl getting all scared." Suddenly Dirk decided he couldn't miss that program for anything. Well, maybe if Celia had been around—

The matches started off with a guy who hid a cigarette lighter in his tights. "He's got a lighter!" Uncle Will yelled. "Why doesn't the ref take it away from him?" Every time the referee looked the other way, the man pulled it out, lit it, and thrust it into his opponent's face. The victim screamed in agony, and so did Uncle Will. "Why can't you see the fire, you fool?" he shouted, but the referee appeared never to figure out what happened. Finally the burned wrestler won. *He'd never have made it without Uncle Will yelling for him,* Dirk thought to himself.

During the next match the good guy was winning when someone handed his opponent a club that he used successfully to win the bout. By the time Uncle Will stopped yelling that time, he was almost hoarse.

The next time the audience's favorite was giving his challenger a thorough beating when the villain pulled something small from his tights and shoved it into his mouth. A moment later he spit purple liquid into the other guy's eyes. The crowd at the wrestling palace, the announcer, and Uncle Will all screamed so loud that Dirk's head began to ache. "It's acid!" the announcer shouted. "It's acid, and it'll blind the man. He'll never be able to wrestle again!"

"Get the police!" Uncle Will yelled. "He can't get away with that." Someone brought a stretcher, loaded the writhing, screaming wrestler on it, and hauled him away.

"How can a terrible thing like that happen?" the announcer screamed. "To ruin a man's life in a fraction of a minute."

"Get the police!" Uncle Will yelled again and again. No one on TV mentioned the police. "If you won't, I will," Uncle Will shrieked. He turned to Dad. "Get the phone book quick!"

Dad flicked off the TV and tried to put his arm over Uncle Will's shoulder. "It's all right," he said softly. "This program isn't any more real than a movie you might watch."

Uncle Will jerked away. "You saw what happened. Get the phone book!"

"Look, Uncle Will," Dad said, "that was all an act. Think about it a minute. If that stuff was strong enough to blind a man, what would it do to the other man's mouth? It would burn the inside. If he swallowed it, it would eat his stomach out. Either way, it would kill him."

The old man sat down, wheezing and looking bewildered.

"I don't think that's a very good program for you to watch," Mom said. "It might cause you to have a heart attack."

Dirk couldn't believe what he'd just seen. Maybe it was just an act. He knew that he'd never seen anything like it. At one point a wrestler had knocked out the referee before he used a club on his opponent. In the sports Dirk had seen or played, you'd be dead meat if you touched a referee.

Mom made some hot chocolate and Dad read them several Psalms from the Bible. Then they all went to bed. Even with all that calming down, Dirk had a tough time falling asleep.

The next morning no one mentioned the wrestling matches, but Dirk thought about them. He had to agree with Uncle Will. It sure looked real, and he'd never seen an announcer get so excited—and so often.

The following Monday morning Dirk gazed anew at Celia. Everything about her was perfection, from her bright hair to her tiny ankles. He wondered how she could be so beautiful and still act so ordinary. With her looks, she shouldn't have to even associate with all the plain-looking kids in the world—like him. That afternoon when Celia got the only A in an algebra test, Dirk groaned out loud.

Her emerald eyes jerked to his. "What happened?" she asked. "Are you all right?"

Her voice, which had a slight huskiness in it, caused his heart to do a flip. He nodded. "I just wondered how you got that A. I thought it was a hard test."

She laughed. Her laugh had that little hoarseness too. "Maybe it depends how hard a person studies." Dirk had never heard such a delicious voice.

He ducked his head to hide his feelings. "Yeah, you probably studied more," he mumbled, picking up his ball-point pen.

When Dirk arrived in the gym that afternoon, he found Donna, all dressed for PE, dribbling across the floor, making one basket after another. When he ran out onto the floor, she passed the ball to him. He missed the basket and quicker than anyone he'd ever seen, she snatched the ball and passed it right into his hands. That time he made the basket.

"You're pretty good," he heard himself tell her. "Where did you learn to play like that?"

She spun the ball on her finger a moment, then flipped it under her arm and smiled at him. "My big brother used to make me play with him all the time. Now he plays on a college team."

"Why can't you play on the girls' team?"

She raised her eyebrows. "Pine Crest doesn't have a girls' basketball team."

"Oh. Can't you play volleyball?"

Donna laughed. "I'll drop basketball and play volleyball if you will."

Slowly it sank in. She loved basketball as he did so nothing else would do. He shook his head. "I guess I understand. Hey, what are you? A senior?"

She laughed. "Hardly. I just turned 15 last week. I'm a sophomore."

Dirk shoved down his rebellious cowlick. "Oh. Sorry. You're pretty tall for a girl."

"Why don't you guys want me to play?" she asked. "Don't you like girls?"

It wasn't that. He knew it wasn't that. All the guys liked girls. They were crazy about them. Most of them didn't do anything about their interest, but just the same—

He grinned. "We like girls. I don't know why we don't want you on our team." Suddenly he laughed out loud. "Maybe you're too good."

She passed the ball between her legs and completely around her body as she dribbled. Then she spun it on the tip of her index finger, looking deep into his eyes. "Did you notice how dumb that sounded?" she asked. "Have you ever wanted to keep any boys off the team because they were too good?"

The coach's whistle stopped their conversation. Everyone ran to the center of the floor. "Same teams as yesterday," Brimley bellowed, "except Kind and Ward trade places."

Dirk had almost been hoping he'd be on her team that day, but he switched as the coach had asked. He probably wouldn't have been brave enough to give her the ball anyway. The guys on her team played keep away with her as the other side had the last time. *Pretty dumb*, Dirk thought. Again, Dirk's team won. She was so good that if either team had played with her rather than against her they'd have won by big numbers.

Brimley signaled them to the bleachers on the west side of the gym and took a position on the floor in front of them. His face looked like a slab of granite. "I wasn't very happy when they told me I had to let a girl play on our team," he bellowed, "and I don't know whether it's right. But you idiots have sure taught me something in the last two days. I learned that every one of you would rather lose a game than have a girl on your team." He drew in a big breath. "Why?" he yelled angrily.

CHAPTER

4

The coach glared in turn at each of the boys, his face red. No one answered.

"I'll tell you why," he shouted. "You all think you're better than girls! Well, I have news for you. This girl is far better than most of you, maybe all of you. I thought we all wanted the best team we could put together. Donna's going to play on this team, and the first idiot who tries anything will be off it—for the season." With a loud snort he stalked off to the shower rooms. The boys stared at each other in shocked silence, then one by one they got up and skulked back to the locker room. Dirk secretly agreed with Mr. Brimley, though he wasn't sure he'd admit it to the other boys.

That night Ron helped Dirk put the last new part on the go-cart, and together they fired it up. Dirk grinned, unable to believe the sound it made—it sounded like a million bees buzzing.

"Where can we drive it?" Ron yelled into Dirk's ear.

Dirk thought a moment. The northwest corner of their place had been left natural—meaning weeds, bushes, and scraggly trees still covered it. The family called the area "the woods." "Let's take it out to the woods," Dirk said. He jumped into the cart and shoved the gas pedal to the floor. The cart took off like an Indy racer, barely missing a lilac bush, an empty bird bath, and the bikes the boys had dumped in the driveway.

"Slow down!" Ron yelled, but Dirk could think only of steering the thing away from trees and other objects.

When he reached the woods, he finally remembered to let up on the gas and slowed to a stop. Ron appeared beside him. "Wow, you're braver than I thought," he shouted over the engine noise. "I'm almost afraid to drive that thing. It may have too much power for us."

His knees still shaking, Dirk climbed out. "Naw. It handles like a rocking chair," he said over the racket. "Go on, give it a try."

Ron took off as gently as the rocking chair Dirk had mentioned. As he watched his friend cruise around the weeds and brush, Dirk decided they should build a race track. He'd use the Rototiller to scratch away the weeds. Then he'd figure out how to flatten the ground. He went after the tiller while Ron drove the cart around the brush.

It took until dark, and wore both boys out, but they carved out a track six feet wide and several hundred feet in circumference.

"What were you doing out there, putting in a garden?" Uncle Will asked when Dirk returned from his shower.

Dad laughed. "You've forgotten about boys, Uncle Will. They'd never work that long on a garden. They were attending strictly to monkey business."

Mom agreed. "Besides," she added, "we won't be putting in a garden for over a month yet."

Finally Dirk got a chance to answer. "We're building a go-cart track," he explained. "We got the weeds out. All we need now is to make it smooth and hard—somehow."

"Well, let's see," Uncle Will said, thinking hard. "Seems to me, you'd use water to do that."

"Why not a lawn roller?" Dad asked.

Dirk decided to use the lawn roller then water the ground down. That ought to make it hard enough. It might even rain so he wouldn't have to set out the hose and sprinkler.

The next day Celia asked Dirk if he'd like to have her help him with algebra. Not only was he flustered talking to her, he was so embarrassed by the insinuation that he wasn't all that smart that he turned red and muttered some vague excuse why he didn't have time. Afterwards he hated himself for missing the chance to be with her. What did it matter who helped whom?

Later, putting on his basketball uniform, he decided he'd help Donna play the very best she could. He'd do that not only to avoid getting kicked off the team, but because it was fair.

As they began practice, Donna happened to be in perfect position to make a three point shot, but rather than pass to her, Bruce handed off to Joey, who, desperately trying to keep it away from Donna, accidentally threw it out of bounds.

Mr. Brimley's shrill whistle stopped the action. "You can go shower down, Bruce," he bellowed. "You just resigned from the team for the year. And you're off for a week, Joey."

Bruce raced halfway across the floor, then returned to within four feet of Brimley. "You better think that one over, coach. No one but you wants a girl on the team." Then he sprinted for the locker room.

After that Donna got the ball her share of the time and made a third of the points for her team, which won 34-14. After practice the boys marched off, chattering like a pack of monkeys. No one said a word to Donna, not even Dirk, although he felt guilty already.

Later that afternoon Dirk went looking for Uncle Will. Finally he checked the back porch. There he found Uncle Will, dressed in a tan suit, light cream shirt, and dark brown tie, sitting on the porch rocker painting shoes with shiny black lacquer. "How does that look, John?" he asked Dirk. "I gathered up all the shoes I could find. No sense doing just one pair."

Dirk stared at them. Under all that black stuff he recognized his white Reebok basketball shoes that had cost $97 three months earlier. Mom's white with blue trim Nikes sat beside Dirk's, and Dad's beside hers. The boy's stomach did some kind of a lurch inside him. "How long will that stuff stay on?" he asked.

Uncle Will's grin spread all over his face. "Don't you worry about this coming off. They call it permanent, and that's exactly what it is."

Opening the kitchen door, Dirk started to slip through it. "The thing is," he said softly, "I'm not sure those shoes are supposed to be black."

Uncle Will's face whipped toward him, the smile intact. "That's what's so great about this polish," he said. "These shoes were all a filthy gray color, but don't worry, this stuff covers anything." He picked up one of Dad's Nikes. "Would you believe I put only three coats on that? Looks like a new shoe, doesn't it?"

Wondering what his parents would think, Dirk escaped into the kitchen. Maybe they'd quit laughing at Uncle Will's tricks now.

Ron came over to work on the go-cart track, and Dirk told him what Uncle Will had done. The boy doubled over with laughter.

"It might not be so funny if they were your shoes," Dirk told him. But they soon forgot all about the shoes and rolled the long track until it felt smooth and solid beneath their feet.

The shoe polishing episode upset Mom a little, but Dad only laughed. When Uncle Will saw Dad's reaction, he turned away and said, "I don't understand why you're laughing. I did the best I could, and if I do say so myself, it's a pretty good job. I guarantee it'll never come off."

At that Dad burst into laughter again, and Uncle Will hurried off to his room with a hurt expression on his face.

After worship that night Dad tried to explain to his uncle that the shoes weren't meant to be polished, but the old man was so depressed that he didn't listen. "I just won't do them anymore since I didn't do well enough." He looked sad for a moment, then smiled. "But you'll see after you wear them awhile."

Dirk took in Mom's sickly green face and found himself laughing along with Dad. It really was funny. But Uncle Will's face collapsed until he appeared ready to cry. The laughter died in Dirk's throat.

"I'm going to bed," Uncle Will said in a hoarse voice. "I can tell when I'm not wanted." The old man left the room, not exactly stooped, but not as proud and erect as usual.

Mom looked from Dad to Dirk. "I suppose we have to feel sorry for the villain now—the one who wrecked over $200 worth of shoes in 15 minutes." But after a short silence, Dirk saw his mother's eyes begin to twinkle, and they all laughed together, trying hopelessly to keep it quiet enough that Uncle Will wouldn't hear.

Later, when Dirk lay in bed, he asked his Heavenly Father to take Uncle Will somewhere else— anywhere else.

The next day at school Celia again offered to

help Dirk with his algebra, and this time he accepted. At least he'd have a chance to get acquainted with her.

"It may take a while," she said, "but I know I can help you understand so well that you won't need any more help. Should I come over to your house?"

His excitement instantly died. He wasn't about to let her meet Uncle Will. He shook his head. "Maybe I should come to your place. I could come after school today."

She frowned and licked her lips. "The thing is," she said slowly, "I'm not allowed to have anyone over until Mom gets home at 6:00."

Dirk felt disappointed too. But he simply would not take her to his house while Uncle Dirk was there. She'd think his family was the missing link. Then he had a thought. "I have to stay for basketball practice. Maybe we could work in the library after that."

She agreed to remain after school, and he noticed her standing at the edge of the gym watching the team play. He passed the ball to Donna whenever she got into position, and she usually scored. But for some reason he could hardly hit the backboard, let alone the basket.

"What's the matter, Ward?" Ron yelled when Dirk blew both free shots after a foul. Dirk wasn't about to admit that not only were his knees shaking, but also his heart.

After Dirk showered, he and Celia hurried to the library. Although she laughed at his mistakes and told him several times how slow he caught on, she really did help him understand the equations. Better than anyone else had.

"Thanks a lot," Dirk said when they finished.

Celia laughed. "I'd do it for anyone as dumb as you if he were as good-looking as you."

Dirk laughed with her but he felt hurt. That's

why he'd resisted her help in the beginning. He didn't want her to find out how stupid he actually was.

"Donna says you're one of the good guys," she said when she finished laughing at her own joke.

"She does? Well, that's only because most of the guys act like jerks. I guess I'm not all that much better, although I can admit that she's one of our best players."

Celia nodded then laughed. "It's hard to say that about a girl, isn't it? But she says you're not like the others."

He grinned. "I wish."

She gathered up her books. "I have to go. Maybe I'll watch you practice again. If you could handle algebra as well as you do that basketball, you'd be OK. Anyway, I'll be at the next game."

Dirk followed her out the door. "Thanks for helping me. You're better than the teacher—and a lot prettier." Feeling his cheeks turning red, he vanished down the hall.

Ron had waited to ride home with him. "Today in practice, you couldn't have hit a train if it had stopped in front of you," he announced with a wide smile. "I just figured out why."

"Yeah?" Dirk poured on the power as they flew down the road.

"Yeah." Ron gulped in a couple of puffs of air. "Celia. I'm glad she decided to wreck your practice today rather than our game with Monroe."

Dirk pushed hard and didn't answer, but he agreed. Celia had made him almost forget the name of the game as well as how to play it.

The ringing of the phone greeted him as he hurried inside the house. It was Mom telling him that she and Dad would be an hour late, and for him to get a rice casserole from the freezer and put it in the oven.

After doing it immediately, he set the oven timer, then changed into his grubbies. He and Ron planned to work on the go-cart track again. They hoped to finish it in another day or two so they could do some serious practice driving.

Ron loped across the road as Dirk came down the steps, and together they trotted around the house and toward the track. Soon Dirk noticed hoses strung across the place, one after another. His eyes followed them until they stopped at a tall man dressed in a navy blue suit. Uncle Will! And he had the end of the hose in his hand, shooting a heavy stream of water over the go-cart track.

"Let's go," Dirk said softly, hurrying toward the elderly man. When they reached him, Dirk noticed that water flooded the track almost all the way around, and that the force of the spray had gouged lots of holes in the dirt. Uncle Will stood in several inches of water and several mud spots soaked through his suit into the snowy white shirt. Muddy water had found even the bright blue tie. "I think that's enough water," Dirk said, trying to rescue the hose from Uncle Will.

The old man jerked the hose back and turned it onto the track again. "It's almost enough," he said with a knowing look. "We just need a little more to the left."

"You're standing in water," Dirk said.

Uncle Will nodded energetically. "Right. And not a drop is getting through that lacquer I put on the other day." To demonstrate how the polish worked, he marched right onto the slippery track. "See?" he asked, turning back to make sure Dirk watched. When he twisted, his feet flew out from under him, and he fell into the mud and water. The hose, still grasped tightly in his right hand, squirted almost straight into the air, giving him a heavy cold shower in the face.

Dirk jumped into the water and threw the hose away so the water sprayed away from them. "Are you all right?"

Uncle Will tried to get to his feet, but kept slipping in the slimy mud. Ron jumped in, too, and together the boys helped him to dry ground where he wobbled but stayed on his feet. "Are you all right?" Ron asked.

"Of course, I'm all right. If you'd left me alone, I wouldn't have even gotten wet." He waggled a bony finger toward the still squirting hose. "Get that and wash me down," he said.

"But that water's cold," Dirk protested.

The old man started after the hose so Dirk dashed across the sodden track and brought it back. "You really want me to squirt this on you? Why don't you go into the house and take a shower?"

The old man grinned. "What would your mother say if we dripped this stuff all over her carpet?"

Dirk ran and turned the pressure down, then directed the stream on his great-uncle until the water ran clear. The old man didn't flinch.

When Dirk finished, Uncle Will reached for the hose again. "Now I'll wash you down," he said, fitting the action to the words. Dirk wanted to yell from the cold water but couldn't let himself because Uncle Will hadn't said anything. When the old man finished hosing Dirk, he washed Ron off too.

As the three hobbled back to the house in their soggy clothes, they all laughed together. Dirk began to see the humor in their escapade and wondered if maybe Uncle Will might turn out to be a pretty good egg after all. Then he remembered the ruined go-cart track.

"We'll have to shower," Uncle said.

Dirk almost growled. As if he needed to be told that.

When Dirk emerged 20 minutes later, he

smelled the casserole cooking. He'd never felt hungrier in his life.

"Feel better?" Uncle Will asked. The old man wore a stone-gray suit, lighter gray shirt, and black tie. "That hot water felt all right, didn't it? I guess we got colder than we thought."

After Uncle Will made sure they had both washed their hands with soap, the two set the table and made a tossed salad together. "Let me make the salad dressing," Uncle Will said. "I have this great recipe in my head." Dirk brought lemon juice, salt, crushed dill seed, and the other ingredients Uncle called for. He could imagine the mess they were fixing, but he didn't care. His parents needed to know what a crackpot they'd taken in.

Dinner steamed on the table when Dirk's parents arrived, and they all enjoyed the meal, including the fantastic salad dressing Uncle Will had made. While they ate, Uncle Will and Dirk told about their hilarious experiences watering down the go-cart track. Both Mom and Dad laughed generously at the story.

Later that night after worship, Uncle Will disappeared but returned in a few minutes carrying a green laundry basket of clothes. He held up something that looked like navy blue pants that would have fit a 6-year-old. "Anyone know whose these are?" he asked.

Mom lowered the paper to her lap so she could see. "Nobody I know," she said. "Where did you get them?" Her eyes returned to the newspaper.

The old man didn't answer but stooped to the basket and lifted a tiny wrinkled brown suit coat. "Who does this belong to?" he continued.

Mom jumped up and snatched the jacket. She glanced at it, dropped it into the basket and examined another, then some gray pants, a light gray coat, finally more pants. Every garment looked as if it would fit a small boy. Whirling around to face Uncle Will, her eyes filled with both anger and tears. "What did you do?" she demanded.

He looked totally baffled. "I put my wet suit in the washer, then I decided it wouldn't be economical to wash so few clothes, so I got some suits from John's and Dirk's closets. Thought I might as well do them all at once." Mom opened her mouth but nothing came out. She did it again and started waving her arms. Her face looked as if it were severely sunburned. But still she didn't say anything.

Dad jumped up and looped an arm over her shoulders. "Come on, Angel, let's go upstairs. We'll talk about this later." He tried to move her toward the stairs, but she refused to budge.

"I don't understand what happened," Uncle Will said. "Did I ruin something?"

Mom finally found her voice. "Only every suit you washed!" Grabbing a light blue suit coat from the basket, she held it by its shoulders. It had once been Dad's. "Who do you think's going to wear this mess?"

Uncle Will's shoulders drooped and his face aged 10 years. Dirk's heart tried to go out to the man, but his own anger wouldn't let it. Two of those ruined suits belonged to him, and he didn't have any others. But that didn't really matter. If he'd had more, they would have been in that basket all shrunk up too. Besides the destroyed suits, several shirts lay in the basket, all a muddy gray color as well as being covered with lint and threads from the ruined suits.

"Is this the kind of thing you've been doing?" Mom said, her voice trembling. "Is this why you can't live alone anymore?"

Uncle Will didn't answer. He just looked grayer and even older.

"All right," Dad's semi-calm voice intervened. "We're not going to say another word about this until morning. Let's all go to bed now and try to get a good night's sleep." The muscles in his upper arm rippled as he tightened it around Mom and steered her up the stairs.

When they disappeared, Dirk glanced back at Uncle Will, who still watched the stairs as though he expected them to reappear any minute. Dirk wanted to bolt upstairs after them, but felt he'd been assigned to care for the old man.

Finally Uncle Will's faded eyes swept around until they met Dirk's. He shook his heavy white hair. "Rats!" he spat out. "And I was just starting to like it here." Lifting his chin into the air, he marched past Dirk to his bedroom.

Slowly Dirk climbed the stairs.

The next morning he awakened early and hurried downstairs. Mom and Dad, already at the breakfast table, looked glad to see him. He wondered if Uncle Will would be gone when he got home that night. In a way he felt sorry for the old man, but only after Uncle Will left could he have a normal home again.

"Sit down," Mom said, setting a bowl of steaming apple-cinnamon oat bran at his place. "We need to talk before Uncle Will gets up."

Dad asked God to bless the food and each of them, especially Uncle Will.

"Is Uncle Will going to a nursing home?" Dirk asked when his father said amen.

"I can't do that," Dad said, shaking his head. "That would be inviting him to die." He sat with bowed head for a moment. "I just can't do it," he repeated.

"We've decided that I'll quit work until school's out," Mom said. "Then you'll take care of him. It's quite obvious he has to be watched every minute."

"But you love to work," Dirk said. "You can't just quit. That's sacrificing your life."

Mom smiled and ruffled his hair. "It's only for a

couple of months, Lamb. And since I work for our own business, I can do a lot of it at home. Then when school's out, you'll be the one sacrificing."

Dirk brushed his hair back into place. "Maybe I'm not willing to do it. He's not *my* uncle! Besides I need to work this summer too."

Dad's eyes grew serious. "Remember, 'If you do it for the least of these you do it for me?' " he said, his eyes searching Dirk's. "We can't do less, Dirk. We can't do less."

As Dirk felt his mouth tighten into a straight line, he told himself that maybe Mom was willing to put her life on hold, but he wasn't. He had lots of things to do this summer.

Angrily he walked out the door.

That night Dirk found another $50 bill on his pillow. He shoved it into his dresser drawer. *As if that would pay for even one suit!*

That week when Dirk prepared for church his anger toward Uncle Will for shrinking his suits returned. But finally he managed to calm himself enough to choose a light yellow shirt and his best jeans. He had no idea what he'd say if someone asked why he'd dressed so casually.

When Uncle Will saw him, his heavy white eyebrows shot up. "I don't like to interfere, John," he said, "but don't you think you'd be more comfortable if you dressed up a little? Maybe put on a suit and tie?"

"What am I supposed to wear, my basketball uniform?" Dirk asked much louder than necessary. "I'm not too crazy about going to church in grubbies, either, but you wrecked my suits. I didn't have a dozen like you. And I'm not John."

As the old man's shoulders slumped, Dirk felt ashamed. He had brought up something that should have been already settled. In its way it was as bad as what Uncle Will had done to the suits.

After Sabbath school, the leader asked Dirk to stay and talk a minute. "I was just wondering when you folks could handle another invasion of the youth group. Your house is about the only one big enough, and your parents help us have a lot of fun when we get together."

Dirk shook his head. "I'm afraid we can't do that anymore right now," he said. "Sorry." He edged toward the door. "I better get upstairs so I can find Mom and Dad," he added, then bolted from the room.

That night Uncle Will convinced Dad that he should watch wrestling again When he saw the "blinded" man performing as always, he agreed that it was all fake and turned off the TV himself.

A week later Donna played in her first basketball game, and Pine Crest won 97-38, the most decisive victory the school had ever achieved. And that was despite the fact that Celia sat on the sidelines yelling her head off and making Dirk almost forget the game. Afterward he was the only player who told Donna how much she'd added to the team.

It was also the last game of the season. The coach said they'd have been in the state tournament if she'd come six weeks earlier. Dirk believed it.

During spring break Dirk carried tools and materials to three guys working for his father as well as drilling countless holes in studs. He didn't mind working hard because it helped him not to think about Celia. Somehow he missed seeing her even though they still didn't talk much to each other. At the end of the week he had enough money to pay Uncle Will back the $50 he'd "borrowed" to fix the go-cart. And he had some left over to put into his savings account.

But Uncle Will didn't see it that way. "You didn't borrow any money from me," he said. "What do you think I am, senile? I don't need any charity, either. I worked hard all my life, and I don't need your money." Pausing, he cocked his head and looked into Dirk's eyes. "An attorney does work hard, you know, and so does a judge."

Dirk slipped the $50 bill into his pocket. "Which was the most fun, Uncle Will? Being an attorney or a judge?"

The furrows in the man's forehead deepened as he leaned back in the rocker and arranged his left foot over his right knee. "Both are fun, John," he finally said. "Are you thinking of going into law?"

Dirk shrugged off a momentary irritation at being called by his father's name. "I haven't decided what I want to do yet. I might like being an attorney."

The faded blue eyes brightened noticeably. "If you take law, I'll pay every dime of your education. All seven years."

Later Dirk told Dad about the conversation. "That's exactly what he told me when I started considering a career," his father said. "He'd really do it for you, too."

Dirk didn't know what he wanted to do after college, but right now he couldn't wait for spring break to end so he could see Celia.

The girl seemed to be happy to be back to school too. Anyway, she made excuses to talk to him a couple of times that day. "Why don't you join the drama club?" she whispered during civics class. "We're about to choose the cast for our final production of the year. We have lots of fun."

He'd join anything to be with her. "Yeah, I might," he whispered back. "When does it meet?"

"Right after school on Mondays and Thursdays."

A rock dropped into the middle of his elation. "How come? The track team meets after school."

She shrugged and her eyes truly sparkled like emeralds. "I don't make the schedules. I guess we're supposed to choose what we want to do."

He spent the rest of the class period trying to figure out what to do. While he knew he'd have a great time with Celia, he'd sort of committed—no, he *had* committed himself to going out for track with Ron. The two were so closely matched in size and skills that they made everything interesting for each other. His friend would consider him a traitor if he changed his mind now. Dirk had to try for track.

The track program had started before spring break but it lunged into full speed the first day school reconvened. Dirk planned to try out for the 200 and 400 meter sprints and the long jump. Anyway, he ran pretty fast and jumped fairly well, so he decided to try those events, maybe more.

When he reached the oval track he found Donna already there. "I'll race you around," she called.

He darted to the lane beside her. "Two laps. One, two—"

"Three and go!" she yelled, starting a fraction of a second ahead of him. He discovered he had all he could do to keep her from increasing her lead as they tore around the oval. Giving his all, he'd nearly caught her when they passed the starting place. He could beat her—he'd just have to push himself harder. When they reached the starting line again, it looked so close he couldn't call it.

You beat," she yelled, trotting a little farther ahead, then bending over to cool down slowly. Watching her, he realized she'd given it all she had and a little more too. The girl definitely had spirit.

"No, I didn't," he answered. "But I would have if we'd gone two more laps."

She straightened up. "Let's go for two more laps then," she wheezed.

Dirk laughed. "You want to make the team or not?"

When she slumped to the grass, he eased down beside her, and they talked about what they hoped to do in track. She hadn't thought about jumping, but when she heard he was trying, she said if he could do it, she could too.

The boys and girls practiced together, and Dirk couldn't believe how well Donna did in the long jump, especially considering she hadn't been working on it.

"See you tomorrow, Ward," Bruce called as he took off.

A few minutes later Ron came after Dirk, and they trotted from the field. "See you tomorrow, Wart," Donna said.

Dirk jerked around to tell her his name was

Ward, not Wart, but the sparkle in her eyes assured him she knew. "Bye," he yelled and continued on his way.

"Donna likes you," Ron said when they were about halfway home. He gave one of his cackling laughs as if it were the funniest thought ever.

Instantly Celia jumped to life in living color before Dirk's eyes. He saw the long light-blonde hair with reddish streaks, and deep green eyes, laughing through long dark lashes. "Forget Donna," he said. "She's just another guy. And not the best-looking one I've seen, either."

When he went inside, he found Uncle Will vacuuming the living room. "Looks as if you're having fun," Dirk shouted over the vacuum roar.

Uncle Will looked up with a wide smile. "Just giving Esther a hand. She's pretty busy this afternoon."

"Good for you," Dirk said and hurried on out to the kitchen where Mom vigorously kneaded a big bunch of bread dough. "Ummm. Smells good, even raw. It's been forever since you made homemade bread."

When she glanced up, Dirk saw that she really was enjoying herself. "It's been forever since I had time for anything special. I thought I might as well make my time baby-sitting Uncle Will worth while."

"Did you put him to vacuuming?"

She nodded and kept going plop, push, plop, push. "He was tickled to help. I'll have to think of some more jobs he can do." Her hands kept pushing and turning the yeasty-smelling dough.

Dirk began to feel hungry. "He thinks you're Aunt Esther, too. She's been dead so long I barely remember her."

Mom's hands stopped, and she leaned on the dough. Her smile disappeared. "I know. Almost eight years. But it must not seem so long to him. As you get older the years pass faster. And not having children probably made them extra close. He talks about her once in a while, and he still loves her with all his heart." She turned the ball of dough, doubled it over again, and pushed.

"Some parts of life are sad," she said softly, almost to herself. "Sometimes he knows they'll be together again one day. Then there are the other times."

Ron came over while Dirk shot some baskets before supper. "Duchy's gone," he said. Duchy, his monstrous golden St. Bernard dog, lived in a chain-link-fenced yard.

"Where could she go?" Dirk asked. "She could never get out of that cyclone fence."

His friend shrugged. "She was there this morning, and now she isn't. I'm not sure she got out alone. Someone may have taken her."

Dirk thought a moment. "What are we going to do?" he asked, taking it for granted that he'd help his friend search for the dog.

"I don't know. Call the cops?"

"Let's make some signs and put them up on telephone poles," Dirk suggested. "I have some heavy paper." The boys went inside, made the signs, and rode their bikes around the neighborhood tacking them up. Then they searched for several miles, calling the dog, but didn't find her.

They'd barely returned to Dirk's yard when Uncle Will ambled down the sidewalk in a jet black suit, a wide smile firmly in place. "Are you boys ready to start up the soapbox cart?"

"It's a go-cart, Uncle Will," Dirk replied absently.

"Well, whatever. I checked the track today, and it looks ready. Are you going to let me try it out?"

Dirk glanced at Ron, who smiled for the first time since he'd come over. The other boy nodded.

"Sure, you can drive it," Dirk said. "If you're sure you won't get hurt."

The old man grinned again. "Get hurt?" he asked. "I've been driving since long before you were born. Let's get that thing cranked up."

Ron helped Dirk pull it from its corner of the garage and started the engine. "Be sure not to give it much gas until you've driven it awhile," Dirk yelled over the loud buzz of the motor, remembering his own first wild ride.

Uncle Will nodded. "Just show me how," he said, folding his long body and legs into the cart. Dirk pointed out the pedals and explained what each did. Then he stepped back and held his breath, expecting anything.

Uncle Will started the cart slowly. As it eased over the grass toward the track, he held up a thumb, looking elated. The track had hardened into a semblance of a race course, though no one had filled the holes. Gradually he increased his speed until he buzzed around the oval, going faster each lap.

Dirk began to fear for his uncle's safety but finally the go-cart slowed and coasted to a stop directly in front of him. The old man unwound his long legs and climbed out, rubbing his hands together. "I can't remember when I've had that much fun," he said gleefully. He motioned toward the cart. "Let's see if you boys can do as well."

Ron took a seat. "I'm sure I can't drive like you, Mr. Ward," he said. "All your years of driving helped you." He made a dozen laps but not as fast as Uncle Will.

Then Dirk took his turn. He wasn't going to let anyone beat him. After all, it was his cart wasn't it? His head jerked back as he shoved the gas pedal in. This time it didn't scare him, and he buzzed around the track faster than anyone.

On the fifth lap he wandered into the spot where

they'd all waded after Uncle Will's fall and lost control of the steering. When the cart swerved off the track and hit the dried weeds, the front wheels flipped into the air and tossed Dirk out on the ground. The cart cleared him before it landed upside down and slid to a stop, the motor still buzzing like a swarming hive of bees. Ron reached inside and killed the engine.

Dirk barely had time to wonder if he was hurt before he felt Uncle Will's gentle hands lifting him to his feet. "You'll be all right, John," the old man said softly. Carefully he brushed the mud and dried grass from Dirk's clothes. Then he grinned into Dirk's eyes. "You sure did drive that machine. At that rate you'll soon be driving in the Indy 500. I have an old stopwatch we can use to time you."

The boys pushed the cart back to the garage and into its corner. Ron looked at Uncle Will with admiration. "You really make that thing go, Mr. Ward. I doubt if I can ever drive it as well as you."

Uncle Will beamed as the boy loped off across the road to his house.

At the supper table Uncle Will told Mom and Dad about their afternoon with the go-cart, and Dirk told them about Ron's missing dog.

The next day Celia again asked Dirk to join the drama club.

"I'd really like to," he said, "but I've already committed myself to track. Besides, I think Mom and Dad would prefer for me to do track."

"But I'd much prefer for you to do drama. It's lots of fun, and no telling how many of us will end up on TV. You'd make fabulous money, Dirk." She tossed her blonde-red hair. "But if you'd really rather please Mommy than me—"

He laughed. "I hadn't thought of that. But really, I already promised Ron I'd go out for track."

Finally he was able to convince her that he couldn't join the drama club.

She turned laughing eyes on him. "I was just being polite," she said. "Really, you'd make a lousy actor. You have to be reasonably smart to succeed as an actor."

He walked off feeling terrible. Maybe she'd felt so disappointed that he didn't choose drama that she couldn't help what she said. Sure. Maybe squash tastes like ice cream too.

Well, he'd just have to figure some other way to be with her. He couldn't invite her to his place because of Uncle Will, and she couldn't have him at her place while her parents were gone. His parents wouldn't let him run around on his bike after dark. They said it would be too easy to get run over. But he'd think of something.

On the way home that afternoon Ron told Dirk that his dog had returned sometime during the night.

When Dirk reached his driveway, he saw a big, short-haired white dog tied to a tree. Dirk couldn't remember ever seeing an uglier dog, but its tail whipped the air, and it pranced on its front feet when it spotted him.

Dirk expected to find someone in the house talking to Mom but only Uncle Will sat in the kitchen while she cleaned the refrigerator. "Whose dog?" Dirk asked, washing a yellow apple.

"Where?" Mom asked, her head inside the refrigerator.

"Out back. Tied to the pear tree."

Mom jerked her head out. "What's a dog doing tied to our tree?"

Uncle Will cleared his throat. "Isn't that your dog, Dirk?"

Dirk grinned at the old man. "Never saw it before." Uncle Will looked crestfallen, and Dirk felt a prick of suspicion. "What do you know about that dog?" he asked.

"I thought you lost a dog."

Dirk could hardly believe his ears. Now Uncle Will was the lost and found department of Pine Crest. "You tied it to that tree, didn't you?"

Are you sure it isn't your dog, John?"

"Ron lost his dog yesterday, Uncle Will, but it came back. It dug under the fence, but Mr. Reed fixed it."

"Whose dog is that outside then?" Uncle Will asked.

Suddenly Mom appeared in front of the old man, her eyes snapping. "Did you tie that dog out there?"

Uncle glanced down and didn't respond.

"He must have found the dog while walking," Mom said. "You'll have to find its home and return it, Dirk."

"How am I supposed to do that?"

"He obviously collected it when he went for his walk. I guess you can walk as far as he did. Just find its owner and return it." She stuck her head back into the refrigerator.

"Come with me, Uncle Will," Dirk said. Maybe the man would at least remember what direction he had walked.

"I'll go with you," he said, jumping to his feet. "I can show you exactly where I found the dog."

"That's the place," Uncle Will said 15 minutes later, pointing to a small mustard-colored house. "It was standing on the lawn over here between the sidewalk and the street."

Dirk swallowed. He'd better make sure. "Let's go ask," he said, heading up the sidewalk. The dog didn't belong there but the woman knew the owner and called the man, asking him to come get the dog.

As they started back home, Uncle Will grinned happily and gave his great nephew his thumbs-up sign. "That turned out all right, didn't it?" Dirk didn't mention that the whole thing needn't have happened at all.

After Uncle Will went to bed that night Mom had a talk with Dad. "It's not enough that I quit work," she fumed, "but now I can't even trust him to go for a walk by himself."

Dad hugged her. "Remember, Rosa," he said, quietly, " 'Inasmuch as you've done it to the least.' Anyway, let him go for his walks. He'll go crazy sitting in the house all day watching you work."

Mrs. Ward thrust her chin out. "I don't know about that, but I'll go crazy having him underfoot every second of the day."

Dad glanced at Dirk. "Let him watch Uncle Will after school."

"He's not *my* uncle," Dirk said. But he managed a weak laugh when he said it.

The next day the science teacher told the class to choose partners for lab. She wanted them to work in pairs for the remainder of the year. Celia slipped into the seat beside Dirk. "I'll be your partner," she whispered. "That is, if you want me to."

"Do dogs have brown eyes?" he whispered back, his heart pounding almost into his back. "Of course I do."

That day Mrs. Waverly assigned cleanup duty to the class. They washed all the beakers, the burners, and the counters, and arranged everything so they could find it. Dirk couldn't remember when he'd enjoyed cleaning so much.

That afternoon Donna appeared as soon as Dirk stepped up to the big oval track. "Still think you can beat me on four laps?" she challenged, her blue eyes sparkling.

"Sure do," he answered, figuring that she had probably been doing some running after school. "If you're sure you want to wind yourself before practice begins."

They stood side by side as before, with Dirk counting. "Three, and GO!" Donna screamed, leaping forward after Dirk had yelled out the first two counts. She led by one stride from the first and held the same lead when they crossed the line the first time. When they reached it the second time Dirk had closed the gap by half, and by the end of the third lap, she was barely in front of him. As they crossed the finish line, Dirk thought they'd tied. This time, he bent over, holding his side. He'd never seen a girl run like that.

"Donna won!" Bruce yelled. At that news Dirk dropped onto the grass and lay still, catching his breath. Donna dropped down beside him, doing the same thing.

"We really tied," she whispered. "He's just giving you a bad time."

Later she almost won the long jump practice. "I'm beginning to think Brimley was right about Donna playing with the girls," Dirk grumbled on the way home.

Ron barked his loud laugh. "Yeah, she's too much for us guys."

Dirk had to grin to himself. He sure couldn't say that she wasn't good enough to play with the boys.

The next day Dirk could hardly wait for science class, but one glimpse of Celia made it worth it. Her soft green skirt and sweater accented her perfect skin, hair, eyes, and teeth. In fact, perfect everything.

The class had collected water from various places to examine under the microscope. Dirk couldn't believe the things they found swimming around in them. When Celia finished examining a drop of mud-puddle water, she raised her laughing green eyes from the eyepiece and met Dirk's for a long moment. He felt his heart melt into a tiny shimmering puddle.

Two afternoons later Dirk found another dog tied to the same pear tree. He'd thought Uncle Will understood that the lost dog was Ron's, and that it had returned. Stomping into the house, he felt angry because he knew that he'd have to go looking for the animal's owner.

"I'm sorry," Uncle Will said as they started down the road. "I thought this must surely be it. It looked as if it had no idea where it was."

"But I told you the lost dog belonged to Ron, and that it returned home. Remember?" Dirk asked as they headed down the road. Fortunately, Uncle Will could walk as fast as he.

Finally the old man stopped. "This is the place."

Sure enough, the dog did belong there, and the woman was so happy to see her pet that she started crying. "You two are an answer to prayer," she said, burying her face into her pet's matted fur.

Dirk didn't tell her that Uncle Will had taken the animal in the first place, and he didn't scold the old man either. The poor guy had enough problems dealing with Mom.

Uncle Will drove the go-cart every time the boys did. In fact, he begged to go play with it more often than they wanted to. But he did a good job and no one had any more problems with the little machine. They used the old man's stopwatch to improve their times and also to see who made the laps the fastest.

Uncle Will won more often than either boy. He even told Dirk that he'd pay for another so they could race. But the boys were too busy and didn't use the cart often enough to warrant the extra expense.

Besides the many showers that Uncle Will still took every day, he stayed in the downstairs bathroom over an hour every morning. "What can he be doing in there so long?" Mom asked.

Dad shook his head. "I don't know, but let him be. At least he isn't dyeing shoes or stealing dogs while he's in there."

But Mom had raised Dirk's curiosity so that night he found Uncle Will alone and asked about it.

"Cleaning my teeth," the old man explained.

"How could that take so long? I clean my teeth at least twice a day, and it never takes longer than five minutes."

"Well, it should," Uncle Will snapped. "If you'd take care of your teeth now, you wouldn't have my problem when you get older."

"What's that?"

Uncle thought a moment. "My dentist told me that unless I take extra precautions, I could lose my teeth within ten years."

Ten years! Dirk thought. *Uncle Will would be dead long before then.* "How old are you, anyway, Uncle Will?"

Mr. Ward nodded. "I'm 87. Too old to start using dentures. That's why I have to go through this ritual every morning. First I floss my teeth with mint floss. Then I use a little round tooth brush to clean between each tooth. Next I use cinnamon floss and the little round tooth brush again. Finally, I use a regular brush, carefully brushing every speck of enamel." His faded old eyes met Dirk's. "It's a pain, John, but when I feel like skipping, I just ask myself if I want to be wearing dentures ten years down the road."

Later Dirk told his father about his talk with his uncle. "Do you think his dentist really told him to go through all that every day?"

Dad smiled and shook his head. "Not if his teeth are good for another ten years. But let him do it. Maybe he feels he's prolonging his life, rather than his teeth. Besides, it's good for him to remember something every day."

One evening Uncle Will handed Dirk another $50 bill. "Only half of it is for you. I want you to buy me stamps with the other half."

"Sure," Dirk said. "But are you sure you need that many? That's a lot of stamps."

Uncle Will nodded. "That's a start," he said thoughtfully. "When I need more, I'll let you know."

Dirk brought the stamps home and took the other $25 to his room. He'd decide later how to spend it though he figured he should save it for sneakers. Mom hadn't bought him new ones after the painting episode, and the guys laughed at his ugly black shoes. Of course, they worked all right, and as Uncle Will said, they stayed black. He just had to wipe them off now and then.

One day Dirk came home late after track and found still another dog tied to the pear tree. "Oh, Heavenly Father," he complained, "what have I done to deserve this? I'll have to spend my evening returning yet another animal." He felt really angry with the old man but not mad enough to tell his mother about it.

After waiting until his mother went to the store, he pounced on Uncle Will. "Why do you keep bringing dogs home?" he asked.

"You mean that one isn't yours? I thought sure it must be. I saw it wander two blocks down the street, watching each car as if expecting someone to stop and pick it up. I took it home before someone stole it."

Dirk sighed loudly. "Get your hat and let's go."

When Dirk untied the perfectly marked black and silver German shepherd from the tree, the big dog jumped against him, knocking him back several feet and scaring him half to death. Then the dog licked his face—from his chin to his forehead in one long swipe.

"You sure he isn't yours?" Uncle Will asked. "I think he knows you."

Without answering Dirk started down the street.

An hour later they returned home, the dog prancing at their heels, as though delighted to be back. Dirk couldn't keep this from Mom and Dad now.

"Are you sure you didn't miss some place he could belong?" Mom asked when he told her about the animal.

Dirk shook his head. "We checked every house for over a mile each way from the place where Uncle Will found him. Maybe I could put up some posters. You know, on telephone poles or something."

"Good idea," Dad said. "And I'll put an ad in the paper."

Uncle Will and Ron helped Dirk make the signs that night. "This is a little different," Ron said with his loud laugh. "I lost a dog, and you found one." He drew the message lightly with a pencil on the big sheet of white posterboard, and handed it to Uncle Will who blackened the letters with a marker. When Uncle Will finished coloring in the letters, he laid the sign on three others he'd already finished.

"Did you notice how gorgeous that dog is?" Ron asked.

Dirk nodded. "Friendly, too. Remember how you felt when Duchy disappeared? Well, I'll bet someone feels pretty awful right now. I asked Mom to cook up a batch of oatmeal after supper. Want to go with me to see how hungry the dog is? He won't eat that stuff unless he's starving."

The dog snarfed up the whole quart of cereal in less than a minute and looked up, wagging his tail. Dirk grinned, his eyes meeting Ron's. "He's starving and wants even more."

"I'll go cook some more," Uncle Will, who'd followed the boys outside, offered.

Dirk shook his head. He wasn't about to let the old man loose in the kitchen. No telling what might happen.

"I'll go get some dog food," Ron said, darting across the road. Dirk approached the dog who lunged at his face again. After shoving him down, he petted the big creature, who sat down and watched him with his big brown eyes. Dirk felt an emotion stirring inside him. It was one nice dog, he thought, as the animal ate a quart of dry food then drank a quart of water.

"That dog's been dumped," Uncle Will said. "He couldn't get that hungry and thirsty in one day."

Dirk nailed seven posters to telephone poles, and his father put an ad in the paper. Then they waited.

Dad brought home a bag of dry dog food and built a long run in the backyard. "He won't need any protection while it's so warm," Dad said. "Of course, his owner will turn up long before it gets cold."

Dirk played with the dog every day. At first he took it for walks but the big animal wanted to run, and he quickly wore Dirk out. Finally Dirk piled onto his bike with the leash in his hand and let the dog pull him 10 miles an hour down the road. The dog also ran beside the go-cart, barking and snapping at Dirk's sleeve as they flew around the track. He paid little attention to Uncle Will, and although Ron tried to get him to chase him, the dog refused, preferring to stay with Dirk.

No one called from any of the seven posters nor the ad.

"What should we do now?" Dirk asked his folks.

"I guess I'll put in another ad," Dad replied. "I don't know what else to do."

"No one's going to answer your ads," Uncle Will said. "Someone dumped that dog."

Dad shook his head. "No one would dump a dog like that."

The old man laughed. "You don't know much about people, John. They're rotten to the core. They get an animal, even a pedigreed one, enjoy it for a while, then grow tired of it and dump it somewhere. The animal usually starves to death or gets run down by cars, but the owner doesn't worry about that."

"Wow," Dirk said, looking at Uncle Will with new respect. "I didn't know you cared that much about animals."

Uncle Will looked mad. "It's people I don't care so much about," he growled. Then his expression softened. "Well, most people are all right," he added.

The next day Dirk found himself telling Donna about the dog while they waited their turns for the long jump. "It's the best-looking dog I ever saw," he said. "I don't know how anyone could dump a dog like that."

"I don't either," she said. "What's the dog's name?"

"Roman," Dirk said without thinking.

"Why Roman?"

"Have you ever heard of a Roman nose? It has a sort of hump in the middle, you know?"

"Yeah. Your dog has a Roman nose, huh?"

His dog? Since when was it his dog? And when did it acquire the name Roman? Dirk grinned foolishly. "Yeah, a little Roman nose. It doesn't hurt his looks though."

Just then Coach Brimley called Dirk for the long jump so he didn't have time to think about it any more until he and Ron rode home.

"I named the dog Roman," he told his friend.

Ron looked surprised. "You're keeping him, huh?"

Dirk shrugged. "I don't know. I don't know why I named him, either. It just happened."

"Hey, that's a good name," Uncle Will said when Dirk announced it at the supper table. "It's a good dog, too."

"I have another ad coming out in the paper, Sunday," Dad said. "You never know when the owner might see it."

Suddenly Dirk's mouth felt so dry that he couldn't speak. At that moment he realized he didn't want to find Roman's owner. The animal had proved over and over that he belonged to Dirk. He pulled only Dirk on a bike. When anyone else took his leash, he sat down. And he bothered only Dirk on the go-cart. Nor did he ever jump on anyone else to give his sloppy kisses. The dog definitely belonged to him.

Secretly Dirk started praying that they wouldn't find the owner, and the following weekend he spent the time during the Sabbath sermon begging God to let him keep the magnificent dog. Sunday Dirk cringed each time the phone rang but the day passed without any calls concerning the big animal.

School went on, and Dirk enjoyed each moment he could spend with Celia. They went to the library to study together whenever they could as well as enjoying their science class. Also they sat together during part of the track meets—the parts that Dirk didn't participate in. Pine Crest High did well—and Donna had a lot to do with that.

Still no one claimed Roman, and he and Dirk grew closer each day. Except for school and church, Roman went everywhere with him. And no more dogs appeared on the scene. Uncle Will apparently felt he'd done his job.

One afternoon Uncle Will called Dirk into his room. "I need your help," he explained. "I'm writing some letters, and I want you to help me figure out who some people are. Sit down, John." Dirk did.

Uncle Will took a rocker in front of him. "Do you remember that cute little girl who sits across the aisle from us in church? The one with the impish blue eyes and soft curly hair?"

Dirk couldn't remember any little girl in the pew across the aisle at all. He shook his head. "Sorry, I guess I didn't notice."

His uncle moved a little closer. "You did too. She sits on the very end of the row right across from me."

Finally it sunk in. The "little girl" uncle referred to must have been 80. "Oh, you mean Mrs. Wilcox. Curly, pure-white hair?"

The old man grinned. "Yeah. That's the one." He scooted his chair back to the table. "Now tell me her first name and her address." His hand poised over his paper, ready to write.

Dirk laughed. "I don't know her first name, let alone her address. You'll have to ask Mom."

Uncle Will whirled around and pointed a long bony finger at Dirk. "You know what your mother would say if she knew what I'm doing. She'd say, 'Uncle Will's really jumped the rail now. We'd better take him to a nursing home.' "

Dirk laughed again and shrugged. "So, how am I supposed to find out? And do you plan to use all those stamps writing to her?"

"No, I'm writing to her once. I want you to find

out the names and addresses of all the other eligible women in the church—from 55 on up. I'll write to all of them, then choose the one I want to marry from the replies."

Dirk thought fast. "I don't think I can help you do that, Uncle Will. Mom would think some of my lights had gone out too. But I have an idea. Why don't you ask Mom for a list of the church members? You can tell from the list which women are single, and the addresses and phone numbers are right there."

Uncle Will stuck both thumbs in the air, then snapped his fingers over his head and twirled a little dance around the room. "I'll do it. First thing you know you won't have to put up with me anymore. I'll be married."

Dirk felt a momentary lift when Uncle Will said he'd be gone. It didn't last long though, as he knew the old man couldn't get married. He also realized that Mom would be ready to do some uncle bashing if she found out what he planned to do. One thing was for sure. He didn't want to be involved. With a shrug he walked off. Uncle Will and Mom would have to settle it between themselves.

The next day Donna brought two big Snickers bars to track practice. "I needed some extra energy," she said, handing him one.

Dirk accepted the candy with a chuckle. "Yeah, thanks. We'll sort of force ourselves to eat them— like medicine." They lolled on the lawn eating the bars and watching the others practice for their events. Ron took part in many of the events, but he had time to kid around with Dirk and Donna once in a while. Most of the boys had accepted Donna but she didn't hang around them much.

Uncle Will brought up the church addresses at the supper table that night and suggested that he might like to write to some of them.

"That's a wonderful idea," Mom said, falling for it all the way. "I happen to have an extra copy of the members' names and addresses. Then you'll begin to get acquainted with some of the people. The roster includes pictures too, you know."

Uncle smiled smugly and took another whole wheat roll.

Before the meal ended, Uncle Will suddenly stared at Mom with disapproval. "I keep wondering why you colored your hair, Esther," he said. "I'll admit it makes you look younger, but I prefer it white. Couldn't you turn it back, just for me?"

Dad almost choked. First on his roll, then with muffled laughter before he regained control of himself. "But I like the color you have on it now a lot, uh, Esther," he said with chuckles bubbling out around the words. "Why don't you leave it that way just for me?"

Mom's cheeks reddened but she didn't answer.

Dirk wondered if Uncle Will did such things just to confuse people. How could he be crafty enough to get that list of church members one minute and all mixed up the next?

Excusing himself, Uncle Will went to his room right after worship that night. Dirk followed him a few minutes later, curious to see what the old man was doing.

"Want to see what I'm writing?" Uncle Will asked, extending a sheet of light-blue paper toward him.

Although Dirk wasn't sure he wanted to, he took it anyway. As he read the precise handwriting, he felt his chest tighten. Uncle Will had asked the women their age, weight, height, income, family situation, and all about their assets. It ended with a request for a recent unretouched picture. Dirk handed the letter back. "The letter's too impersonal," he said, "and nosy. Would you want to reveal all that stuff about yourself?"

Uncle Will read the letter again and nodded. "Sounds good to me too," he said, turning back to the copy he was working on.

Dirk decided to let Uncle Will know how it felt if he would have received such a letter. "OK, how much is your income, Uncle Will? Tell me all about your assets too. I need to know what I'm going to inherit."

The old man's eyes jerked up from the letter. Then he smiled. "Good try, John, but you know better than to ask that kind of question. It's impolite."

A few minutes later Dirk left. *Sometimes I might as well forget reasoning with the old man*, he thought to himself.

The next day at an assembly in the auditorium the principal announced the athletic awards banquet. Dirk sat back smugly. Being in track and basketball, he'd be going, and Celia would love to attend with him. Closing his eyes, he imagined the banquet. First, of course, would be the meal. For that he'd better polish his table manners. Everything would have to be just right. Maybe he'd get brave enough to hold her hand when they passed out the trophies and other awards. He'd be extra proud to be with her, the undisputed prettiest girl in school. His thoughts jerked back to the auditorium and he wiped his hands on his jeans. Just thinking about it made his palms sweat, but he didn't get a chance to ask her that day.

The next afternoon the track team bussed 25 miles to Brownleigh for a meet. Pine Crest took the majority of events and climbed back on the bus in high spirits. The kids chanted the school cheer several times as loudly as they could. Then they took turns telling jokes.

"I wanted to go water-skiing over the weekend,"

Ron announced, "but I couldn't find any water with a steep enough slope."

After the groans died down, one of the girls held up her hand. "I found out why Cinderella got kicked off the soccer team," she said. "She kept running away from the ball." Even more groans.

Finally the bus arrived back at the school, the students still in a high mood. Dirk and Ron unlocked their bikes and pulled them from the rack. Before they could leave, however, Donna appeared and asked to talk to Dirk alone for a minute.

"I remembered a joke I wanted to tell but I was too shy," she said. "May I tell you now?"

"Sure."

"Well, there was this guy who really liked a certain girl. He wanted to take her out in the worst way but couldn't get brave enough to ask. Finally he decided it would be easier to ask over the phone so he called her. 'I like you an awful lot,' he said. 'Would you go out with me if I asked?' 'Yes!' the girl said almost before he got the words out. 'I'd love to go.' The guy felt great and mentally congratulated himself. The girl must like him as much as he liked her. She couldn't have been more excited. 'By the way,' the girl asked a moment later, 'who is this?'"

Dirk burst out laughing.

"Now I have a question I'm afraid to ask you," she said when he quieted. "I was wondering if you'd go to the awards banquet with me."

CHAPTER

9

Dirk couldn't believe he'd heard right. She'd said it so softly he had to strain to catch her words. Maybe she really hadn't asked him to the awards banquet. But she had. He'd heard her all right—and wished he hadn't. What could he say? Girls asked guys to things all the time, and he didn't have an understanding with anyone. Suddenly he realized that he should have expected this as Donna didn't have too many friends among the boys.

"Sure," he finally said, realizing the silence had grown long. "That would be just great."

"OK, see you," she said in a dead voice, then dashed off as though she were in a sprint.

He told Ron about it on the way home. "The worst part," he said, "is that I hesitated so long I probably made her feel as bad as if I'd said no."

"What about Celia?"

"I guess I'll have to tell her Donna asked first and see if we can figure a way out."

Dirk thought about Celia as he laid his bike in the grass and went after Roman. He'd been taking the big dog for a run most afternoons lately—though what he actually did was to let the animal pull him on the bike. By the time they went a couple of miles that way, the dog was ready to run alongside on the way back home.

When Dirk returned from the ride, Uncle Will beckoned him into the house. "I have the letters all finished and mailed," he announced.

"Did you take out the personal questions?" Dirk asked.

The old man shook his white head impatiently. "Of course not. I need that information to choose the right woman."

"What if they ask you how much income you have?"

"They won't. What you don't seem to understand, John, is that this is my project. If it were their project they'd ask the questions. Because it's my project, they answer the questions."

"OK, but don't be too surprised if it doesn't turn out as you planned." Dirk went to the kitchen to put some potatoes in the oven.

Dirk couldn't find the right opportunity to bring up the awards banquet the next day, and Donna didn't seem as friendly as usual. Nothing seemed to be going right. He talked Donna into a race that he won for a change, but he felt a chill radiating from her direction.

"Don't worry about it," Ron said when Dirk mentioned it. "I don't have a date at all yet, but I don't mind going stag. I won't have to watch my table manners as much that way."

"You know your table manners are OK anyway," Dirk grouched.

A week later as Dirk and Celia left the science classroom, she turned her ravishing smile upon him. "I keep forgetting to mention the awards banquet," she said. "You are taking me, right? Let's wear matching colors."

His heart dropped into his shoes. After more than a week she gets around to the subject. Since he was stuck with Donna he'd been hoping Celia wouldn't mention it.

He cleared his throat. "Um, well, Donna Kind already asked, and I didn't know what else to do so I accepted. Think I could get out of it?"

For a moment she looked disappointed, then burst out laughing. "That scarecrow?" she squealed. "How'd she ever get the nerve to ask you?"

For some reason Dirk resented Celia's comment about Donna. She wasn't that bad. He shrugged. "We see each other in track all the time, and I'm the only guy who treats her decently."

The petite blonde laughed again. "I guess you can't get out of it now, idiot. You'll just have to give her a thrill. Probably the only date she'll ever have in her entire life. Know what your real name is? Dirk the Jerk." She took off down the hall toward algebra class, still laughing.

Dirk didn't follow. Instead he went to the restroom. He needed a minute to think. Celia didn't even seem to care that he was going with another girl. Maybe she didn't consider Donna a girl, but he did. A really decent girl.

"Hey, I got asked to the awards banquet," Ron said just before they reached home. "Guess who?"

Dirk didn't feel like launching into a guessing game. "I don't know, who?"

"Celia Gould."

Dirk's mouth went dry. He should have known she'd ask someone else. And he should be glad she'd asked his best friend. Ron would never get involved with a girl *he* cared about. But no matter how Dirk looked at it, he wasn't happy about any part of it. But he didn't say anything until they parted company at their houses. Then it was only a crisp, "See you later."

That night he had a talk with himself in which he tried to convince himself that he could handle anything for one evening. And it wasn't even a whole evening, only a few hours. Also he told himself that he had to make sure Donna had a good time. That was his responsibility for the evening, and he'd better get with it.

Dirk tried his best to be relaxed in science lab the next day. He couldn't laugh at Celia's date as she had at his, but he had to be a good sport. After all, he'd accepted a date with someone else first.

Everything seemed to go well until school dismissed. He still didn't feel like riding home with Ron so he rushed to the bicycle stands only to find his friend waiting.

They both unlocked their bikes and hopped on, riding together yet not speaking. The trip home had never seemed so long, and the silence bothered Dirk, but somehow he couldn't break it. When they turned onto the road to their houses, Ron pulled close. "I'm sorry you feel bad about Celia asking me," he said. "If I were making the rules I'd let you take them both, but no one asked me."

Dirk looked into his friend's huge brown eyes to see if he was laughing at him. But rather than appearing amused, Ron seemed troubled. "Look," he said, "the same thing happened to both of us. We got asked and didn't know what to say. You should understand, Dirk."

For a few moments Dirk thought it over, then nodded with an embarrassed grin. How could he be mad at his friend? "Yeah! It's beginning to sink through the old skull. It's not your fault. But hey! Didn't you want to go with Celia any more than I wanted to go with Donna?"

A strained expression on his face, Ron pedaled furiously for a few minutes. "I'd like to say that's how it is," he finally replied, "but the only reason I didn't want to go was because of you. Who wouldn't be proud to go with Celia? She's like a movie star."

He took a deep breath. "But I still couldn't refuse, could I?"

Relaxing on the pedals a little, Dirk smiled back at his friend. "You couldn't refuse, but you didn't have to like it." Then he told Ron about Uncle Will's search for the perfect wife.

A few evenings later Uncle Will invited Dirk into his bedroom. He held up six envelopes. Four white, one pink, and one lavender. "Letters," the old man said, grinning widely. "Every last one of them is from a woman. I waited until you got home to open them."

"Hey! You're afraid to open them."

"Not exactly afraid. I just wanted to share them with you." He shoved one at Dirk. "Here, you read it."

Dirk pushed it back. "No way. You read it to me."

The old man's hand trembled as he tore the end from the envelope and shook out a single sheet of paper. He stared at the paper a moment then handed it to Dirk. "You'll have to read it to me," he said, puffing as though he'd been running. "For some reason I can't seem to focus on the thing."

Dirk opened the paper.

Dear Sir: I'm 77 years old, five-foot-three and weigh 179 pounds. I have only my social security check of $400. I'd be interested in meeting you if you have lots of money. Susan L. Mahoney

Dirk laughed until Uncle Will held up a hand. "But that's exactly what you asked for," he told his uncle.

"Well, I'm not interested in anyone that poor. And she must look like a butterball turkey." He tore the end from another envelope and handed it to Dirk.

Don't bother me anymore, you dirty old man. I'm very disappointed in you. I saw you in church and thought you were a gentleman. Does Mrs. Ward know about the letter you sent me?

When Dirk laughed again, Uncle Will looked more sad than ever. "I only did it so I could get out of your way," he explained. Then an alarmed expression crossed his face. "Do you think she'll tell Esther?"

"Do you mean Mom?" Dirk asked, suddenly irritated.

"I mean my wife." Then Uncle Will looked confused for a moment and shook his white hair. "No—I guess I mean your mother. Will she send me to a nursing home?" Then he remembered the rest of the letters and tore the ends from all of them and handed them to Dirk. "Here, you read these. Maybe one of them would make a suitable wife."

One said she'd be glad to meet Uncle Will, another said she was in a nursing home but he could visit her. A third said her husband might not like for her to make good friends with a senile old man, and the last one was so incoherent that Dirk couldn't figure it out.

"Would you check out the one who wants to meet me?" Uncle Will asked. "Or maybe you could point her out in church."

The boy shook his dark head. "No way. I don't know the woman, and besides, I'm not getting involved in your crazy scheme." He stood. "You can figure it out yourself, Uncle Will, if you just put your mind to it." Then he hurried upstairs to his own room to get busy on his homework.

All too soon the day came for the sports awards banquet. Mom had finally helped Dirk pick out a new navy suit. He kept thinking about Celia's offer to color-coordinate their clothes and wondered if she'd match Ron. The day of the awards banquet Mom brought home a wrist corsage for him to give to Donna. Dirk spent almost an hour getting ready before Ron's mom drove the boys to the school where they were to meet their dates.

Dirk saw Celia first. She looked beautiful as always—and she hadn't coordinated her clothes with Ron. Already Dirk felt better. He'd live through the evening after all. But how would he get to see her during the summer?

10

Then he saw Donna, and his breath left him. Her blue eyes appeared enormous in her heart-shaped face, her pink and cream skin delectable. And her golden hair, pulled to the right side, sent cascades of curls tumbling down almost to her shoulder. Wearing a light yellow dress with some kind of ruffle at the waist, she looked positively glamorous. And not even skinny. As he stared he realized she looked so different because she normally didn't dress up or wear make-up to school. In fact, her hair had always looked nearly uncombed when he'd been with her in basketball and track. Celia always wore makeup and kept every strand of hair in place.

Donna laughed. "Well, shall we go find something to eat?"

Dirk definitely wasn't hungry. "Sure, I'm starved."

He, Donna, Ron, and Celia had been placed together. Ron carried the conversation with his booming voice and funny jokes. Celia didn't like the baked potato so sent her plate back for more entree. While they waited for the new plate, Dirk realized that Donna, even dressed up, still couldn't compare to Celia's extravagant beauty. Even so, no guy would ever have to be ashamed to be seen with Donna.

During the awards presentation Dirk didn't touch Donna's hand once, although to be truthful, he did think about it. His restraint had something to do with being loyal to Celia, he figured. But once, during some funny comment by Coach Brimley, Donna reached over and touched his folded hands.

They finally said goodbye in front of the school where Dad waited to take Ron and Dirk home.

"Did you boys have fun?" Dad asked, signaling left, before pulling into traffic.

"Yeah," Dirk said. Then he realized that he really had had a good time. Donna had been quiet but fun. She'd acted happy to be there and hadn't complained about a thing. Kind of the way she was every day at track. Yeah. He'd had a good time.

Mom met them at the back door, sparks shooting from her eyes. "I've just learned about your letter-writing partnership with Will, Dirk." She bit off the words. "Pastor Miller called and enlightened me. We'll be lucky if we don't all get invited not to return to church anymore."

Dad tried to pull her into his arms but she stiffened and backed away. "Calm down, Love," he said softly. "It can't be that bad." She ignored him, her eyes glaring into Dirk's. "What on earth is the matter, Rosa?" Dad persisted.

She finally faced him, slashing her index finger into the air toward Dirk. "Ask him!"

Mr. Ward turned to Dirk. "Do you know what she's talking about?"

Dirk didn't know what to say. Finally he nodded. "I know, but I didn't go into any partnership, Mom. I tried to get him to change his letter but otherwise I left him alone. Honest."

"Who bought the stamps?" his mother demanded loudly.

"I did." Very quietly.

Backing inside, she let them into the house. Dirk walked through the kitchen into the living room where Uncle Will sat on the couch, his head hanging. He looked as if he'd just been convicted of murder 1. Mom had evidently been working on him before Dirk and his father arrived.

Sitting beside his old uncle, Dad put his arm around the stooped shoulders. "Uncle Will," he said, "maybe you'd better tell me what happened." The white head shook once and sagged even more.

Grasping Mom by the arm, Dad pulled her into his lap, holding her firmly. "Now—woman—tell me what's been going on in the half-hour I've been gone."

Tears bubbled from her eyes and she threw herself against his chest. "It's been going on for days, only we didn't know it," she mumbled against his shirt. "Your totally senile uncle has been writing letters to the church women, and you should see the letters." She took one big sniff. "It seems he's been trying to get married so he won't bother us anymore."

Mr. Ward looked at his once proud uncle, now bent almost double. "Maybe he feels unwanted."

Mom's eyes opened wide for a second but she didn't reply.

Uncle Will lifted his white head and shook it twice. "That's not it at all. Everyone's been plenty good to me. Better than I deserve. But I've never been a burden to anyone before, and I don't like it very much."

"What if we let you help around the place more?"

"I'd know you were making work for me."

"Well, let's have worship and get to bed. We'll talk again tomorrow when we've all had a good night's sleep."

When Uncle Will prayed, he thanked the Lord

for letting him stay there as though the big uproar were all in the past.

When Dirk finally crawled into bed, he could barely remember the awards banquet.

Loud voices awakened him the next morning so he jumped from his bed and into his clothes. Following the racket, he knocked on his parents' bedroom door.

"Your morning greetings are pretty loud," he said when they invited him in.

Mom grimaced. "I guess it's mostly me," she admitted. "I just don't see how we can keep that old man anymore."

Dad dropped an arm over her shoulder. "Remember? 'Inasmuch . . .' Look at it this way, Rosa," he said with a smile, "school's out so you can go back to work. Today, if you want. How's that?"

She looked surprised. "I guess I could. I hadn't thought of that. But I don't trust Dirk with him. He smiles with those watery old eyes, wags a bony finger, and Dirk jumps. No telling what will happen when those two spend all day together."

"Don't worry about it, Mom," Dirk said. "I'll watch him every minute."

"I don't know that I can just run off today without giving it some thought." Then a big smile brightened her face, and she almost ran to her closet and threw the door open. "Oh, why not? I need to get back to work to save my sanity. Dirk, get out of here so I can get dressed. I'm going to work."

Mom and Dad left before Uncle Will came from his room, his white hair damp from his first shower of the day. The old man looked around, then sat down at the kitchen table. "Are they out finding a nursing home for me?"

Dirk laughed. "No, they're out working. Mom went back to work today. From now on, it's just you and me, kid. What do you want for breakfast?"

"You mean they aren't sending me away?"

"As far as I know they're not. But we'd better be careful."

After breakfast Uncle Will wanted to drive the go-cart so Dirk cranked it up for him. They took turns, using the old man's stop watch to declare time winners. Dirk had long since become bored with the little vehicle so he let Uncle win every time. Maybe if he could take it somewhere else he could get interested in it again, but going round on that bumpy little track had definitely grown old.

When he finally got Uncle Will out of the go-cart, it seemed like late afternoon, but the clock read only 10:00. It was going to be a long summer.

"I'm going to be working in the garden until noon," he told the old man, then went after his hoe.

He hadn't finished weeding the carrots before Uncle Will also arrived with a hoe over his shoulders. Together they finished hoeing the garden before lunch. "Thanks," Dirk said as they walked toward the house. "I'd have been out there half the afternoon if you hadn't helped."

After lunch the two sat at the table for a while. "We need a project this summer," Uncle Will said, twirling the saltshaker on its corner. "Something that we'd both be eager to get up for every morning. What do you think we could do?"

What Dirk thought he needed was to get rid of the old man so he could earn some money for school clothes. He'd been working for his father during the summer for two years now, and he enjoyed it. Dirk tried to smile. "I already have a project that's going to last all summer, Uncle Will. It's keeping you out of trouble."

Uncle Will flinched as though in pain. "I don't need a baby-sitter." He sat quietly for a few minutes. "What would you be doing if I weren't here?"

"I'd be working, earning money for school clothes."

"I'll give you the money for your clothes. How much do you need?"

Dirk shook his head. "The folks wouldn't go for that."

"Hmmm." Uncle Will rested his chin in his hands. "I'll help you earn some money then. What can we do?"

"I don't know. I've been helping Dad."

"Maybe we could groom people's horses."

"What? I don't know anyone who even owns a horse!"

Uncle Will blinked his eyes. "Oh. Right. Maybe we could wash cars."

"We could wash a few," Dirk said, "but we don't have many neighbors." Again he shook his head. "And I don't think we could wash enough cars to make any money."

"Maybe we could make bird houses and feeders."

"Wrong season, Uncle Will. You feed the birds in the winter, and they're already nesting by now."

"What about making doughnuts or cinnamon rolls?"

"That might work. If we could find someone to buy them. Have you ever made them?"

Uncle Will shook his head. "But Esther has a recipe, I'll bet. Let's look and make some for supper tonight."

After Dirk gathered up some of Mom's recipe books, they started searching through them. "Here's a cinnamon roll recipe," he said a few minutes later. But when he read through the recipe, he thought it looked pretty complicated. "I don't know if we could do this, Uncle Will. I don't even know what some of the words mean."

"Here's a bunch of doughnut recipes," Uncle Will said.

Dirk read through a doughnut recipe. When he discovered they had to be fried in hot oil he decided to forget them. Someone would get burned for sure. Going back to the cinnamon rolls, he read through the instructions again. "Do you know what knead means?" he asked.

"No, but you have a dictionary, don't you?"

A few moments later Dirk ran his finger down the column until he found the word and read: " 'To work and press into a mass with or as if with the hands.' " He raised his eyes. "That doesn't sound hard. Let's make cinnamon rolls for supper. It'll be a surprise for Mom and Dad; and everyone loves cinnamon rolls. Maybe we can work up a route."

"Or advertise them in the paper," Uncle Will suggested. "We might sell all we can make."

About two hours before the time his parents were supposed to get home, Dirk and Uncle Will washed their hands with soap and started putting the cinnamon rolls together. They read the recipe carefully and did exactly as it said. "This is hard work," Dirk announced when they had the ingredients all in. "Now if we can figure out this kneading stuff. It says knead for 10 minutes."

He turned it onto the floury breadboard and started shaping and pressing as the dictionary had said. "Hey, I know how to do this. I've seen Mom knead bread." Pushing the dough into a big pile, he smashed it down, then folded it over and pushed it down again. In a few minutes he had a rhythm going and continued for the 10 minutes the recipe specified.

When Mom and Dad arrived Dirk and Uncle Will had supper on the table. The cinnamon rolls were finished and frosted as well.

"The cinnamon rolls are great," Mom said later, wiping her mouth with her napkin. "I had a fantastic day, and having supper ready puts the topping on it."

"We thought maybe we'd sell cinnamon rolls," Uncle Will said. "Earn some money for John's school clothes."

Dad shook his head. "No way. We'd end up with a lawsuit when someone found a fingernail in a cinnamon roll. You guys can keep the place up and have the meals ready." He grinned at Dirk. "I promise you'll have something to cover your hide when you go back to school."

"What are we supposed to do all summer?" Dirk asked.

"Learn to play chess—or croquet," Mom suggested.

After worship Uncle Will wagged Dirk into his room. "Want to play chess?"

"I guess. There's nothing else to do."

The old man pulled down a checkerboard and set some strange pieces on it. "I'll teach you as we play," he said. "You play first."

Uncle Will moved each piece in a different way and not always the same. Dirk soon decided his old uncle didn't know any more about chess than he did. As he was figuring a way to quit, Dad called him to the phone.

"I decided you weren't ever going to call," Celia said, laughing. "I guess you aren't going to come over either, huh?"

Dirk sat down on the carpet before his shaking knees collapsed. "I'd like to come, but I don't know exactly when I can. I can't leave in the daytime, and my folks won't let me ride my bike at night."

"I can go anywhere I want before dark. Maybe I can come over there."

No way! He wasn't having anyone over here to see what Uncle Will would do next. "I don't think so. I'm pretty busy."

"Oh. OK, I can take a hint. You don't want to see me."

"I do. I really do. Please don't think that. Maybe I could come over to your place this weekend."

"Maybe. Why don't you call me sometime, and I'll let you know. I'm not sure if I want to see Dirk the Jerk." The phone clicked and began a loud buzz. He hung it up.

CHAPTER

11

That evening Dirk waited until Uncle Will disappeared into the bathroom, then went looking for his parents. "Taking care of Uncle Will is ruining my whole social life," he grumbled.

"I don't understand why," Dad said. "Other kids have old relatives too, you know."

"Not crazy ones!" Dirk snapped. A noise behind him caused him to turn around in time to see the old man disappear down the hall. He'd heard what Dirk said!

A million thoughts raced through Dirk's head. Should he tell Uncle Will he wasn't talking about him? No, he couldn't tell an outright lie—and besides the old man wouldn't believe it. Should he try to convince Uncle Will that he really was crazy? Maybe he'd agree to go to a nursing home. No, he couldn't do that, either.

What he had to do was go face his uncle and tell him he was sorry. And that would be the truth.

"Well," Mom murmured, "what do we do now?"

"I don't know," Dad replied. "But one thing I do know is that having Uncle Will here is as hard on him as it is on us." He hurried down the hall toward the den.

When Dad didn't return, Dirk went to bed feeling terrible. "I'm truly sorry for hurting him with my big mouth, Father," he whispered into the darkness. "But do You think I should have to baby-sit him all the time? Is that Your plan for my summer? He's not *my* uncle, You know." Dirk had a hard time falling asleep.

The next morning Uncle Will didn't come out so Dirk knocked on the den door, then entered at Uncle Will's response. The old man lay in bed looking even older than usual.

Dirk sat in the brown overstuffed chair beside the bed. "I can't tell you how sorry I am about last night. I was just having a fit because Dad wouldn't let me do something I wanted."

Uncle Will didn't respond.

Dirk picked at a crumb stuck to the chair arm. "People say things they don't mean when they're upset. You know that, Uncle Will. Don't you?"

Still no response.

The crumb came loose, and Dirk flicked it off onto the carpet. He'd have to give it everything he had. "Look, Uncle Will," he said with a forced laugh, "that phone call was from a girl. A special girl, and I was trying to get to go see her. Wouldn't you get upset if you liked someone a lot and couldn't see her? But I was mean to take it out on you, and I'm really sorry. Please forgive me?"

A long bony hand snaked across the covers toward him. "Sure. Put her there, pal."

Dirk shook the hand until his arm ached. "Thanks. Now get up so we can do something." He hurried to the kitchen to make pancakes—Uncle Will's favorite. As he poured in the blueberry pancake mix he heard the shower running in the bathroom by the den.

Twenty minutes later Uncle Will sat down and Dirk served the steaming pancakes. "What do you want to do today?" Dirk asked while they ate.

"I want to catch up on my reading while you go see that girl."

Dirk grinned. "Well, to tell you the truth, they won't let me do that."

The old man reared his face up from his pancakes. "Why? Don't they trust you? Oh. I guess it's me they don't trust."

"Maybe they don't trust either of us," Dirk replied, smiling. "How would you like to take Roman for a nice long walk? I mean both of us will go."

Uncle Will nodded. "Sounds all right to me. Better than sitting in a nursing home."

As Dirk attached Roman's leash to his collar, he thought about his great uncle. More and more he understood why Uncle Will didn't want to go to a nursing home. The old man was too interested in life. "Settle down," he told his dog, rubbing the velvety black ears. "We'll be on our way in a few minutes."

"Maybe I should have run him with the bike first," he told Uncle Will as they started down the road with Roman tugging on the leash. "He has more energy than a nuclear plant." Dirk jerked back on the rope several times but the big dog kept right on pulling as though unaware of Dirk's attempted guidance.

"He needs a bit in his mouth," Uncle Will said. "When you jerk back on one of those things, the horse takes notice."

"I know, but they hurt the horse. I don't like that."

Uncle Will nodded, picking up his pace a little. "Right. Maybe if we walk faster, he'll wear out and slow down."

"Sure he will," Dirk said. "In your dreams. That dog can run for miles. But maybe I'll run him a little. You just take your time." He took off down the road with the dog racing ahead at the end of his leash. When Dirk felt he couldn't go another step, he headed back toward the old man. The dog, not even panting, still tugged at the leash.

After a while they came to a crossroads. Dirk saw the small pickup truck coming and stopped at the edge, but Uncle Will evidently didn't notice they'd reached another road where they could expect to see traffic in the middle of the morning. Looking neither left nor right, he didn't slow a bit, but charged right out in front of the truck.

"Uncle Will! Stop!" Dirk shouted.

But the old man didn't hear. The brakes screeched on the black-top and the little truck skidded straight toward Uncle Will who had crossed the center line.

"Uncle Will!" Dirk yelled again. Suddenly Roman hit the end of his leash with such force that it snapped out of Dirk's hand. The big dog bounded across the road, rose up on his back feet, and hit Uncle Will hard in the back. Uncle Will flew off the road into the ditch, just before the skidding pickup slammed into Roman. It pushed the mangled dog many feet down the road before shuddering to a stop.

Dirk couldn't look and his feet wouldn't move. He tried to swallow the huge lump in his throat as he watched the truck driver jump out and, without even glancing toward Roman, run to Uncle Will, stooping over the quiet man.

Suddenly Dirk's body swung into action, but his feet didn't take him to Uncle Will. Uncle Will couldn't possibly be hurt very bad. The truck hadn't touched him. Instead he found himself leaning over Roman. The big dog looked dead. His closed eyes, the blood oozing from his nose and mouth, and one hind leg hanging at a strange angle made Dirk feel like vomiting. The lump in his throat grew until he could barely breathe. Roman had given his life to save a silly old man who didn't even stop to check for cars.

An old man who caused one calamity after another.

"I have a CB in my rig," the pickup driver said. "I'll call for help."

Dirk didn't know what to do so he just stood by his dog, tears streaming down his face until a paramedic rig arrived. After checking the old man over and receiving Dad's name as well as Uncle Will's and their address and phone number, they hauled Uncle Will away. The unit didn't speed and though the lights flashed the siren remained silent.

No one invited Dirk to ride in the ambulance but he wouldn't have gone anyway. He didn't care if Uncle Will died. *Oh please, God,* he prayed silently, *don't let anything happen to Roman. I love him so much.*

Finally he noticed the pickup driver looking at him.

"I'd be glad to haul the dog to a vet if you think we dare put him in the truck," he said softly.

Though he knew you aren't supposed to touch an injured animal or person, Dirk also realized that they couldn't leave Roman lying there. He nodded. "Yes, let's lift him in." After gently placing the still form into the back of the truck Dirk climbed into the passenger seat. Neither said a word until they arrived at the veterinarian clinic.

"Do you want to stay while I examine your dog?" the woman vet asked after the driver had helped Dirk carry Roman into a glaring white room and place him on a high steel table in the middle.

Dirk nodded silently.

"I have to go file an accident report," the driver said, handing Dirk a scribbled sheet of paper. "Here's my name, telephone number, and insurance company. Please call me tonight."

Again Dirk nodded.

"I'm Cindy Stern," the doctor said. "You'd better sit down. You don't look so hot."

Taking a seat, he concentrated on trying to breathe, not even watching to see what she did to Roman. He had no idea how long he sat there. Once he briefly wondered about Uncle Will, but out of the corner of his eye he could detect Dr. Stern doing things to Roman, and he felt only for the dog. Roman was not only his first dog, but the best one in the world. And he'd saved Uncle Will's life. He just had to get well. Again he asked his Heavenly Father to heal his pet.

Finally Dr. Stern sat down beside Dirk. "Roman has several broken ribs," she said. "And his skull is at least cracked. I'll need some X-rays. But I want to start treating him for shock even before the X-rays. Could you call one of your parents to come?"

Dirk looked starkly into her eyes. "Will he die?"

Her lips stiffened, and he could see her carefully choosing her words. "He's a very sick dog," she finally said. "But with the proper care he at least has a chance. It's going to cost a lot of money, and I can't guarantee anything. I need to talk to your parents right away. Please call them, Dirk."

Dirk waited in the reception room until Mom arrived less than a half-hour later. "Dad's with Uncle Will," she said, dropping into the chair beside him. "He's scratched up and badly bruised, but he's going to be all right. They may release him later today. How's Roman?"

Dirk almost felt angry that Uncle Will was OK while he didn't even know whether Roman would live. "He's hurt real bad, Mom. Dr. Stern wants to talk to you right away."

He told the receptionist that his mother had arrived, and the pretty young doctor invited them into her private office. "Please sit down, Mrs. Ward. As I already told Dirk, his dog is seriously hurt with multiple fractures and possible internal injuries. I think we can save him but it'll be very expensive."

"How much money are we talking about?" Mom asked.

Dr. Stern shook her head. "It will involve surgery and at least a week in the hospital. I can't give you a figure, but it'll be more than a thousand dollars." Mom gasped, but the doctor continued, "Whether he lives or not depends a lot on the dog's will. From what I've already learned I'd guess Roman has a great heart."

Mom let out a long, loud sigh, then remained silent for a few more minutes. "I just don't know about spending all that money on a dog," she finally said softly. "It almost seems sacrilegious when there are so many people that need help too."

12

But Mom," Dirk pleaded, tears running down his cheeks, "Roman saved Uncle Will's life." He sniffed and swallowed. "And Uncle Will didn't even look for traffic. That truck was almost there before he ever blundered into the road! I yelled as loud as I could, but he wouldn't stop. It's all that senile old man's fault."

Mom put her arm around him and pulled him close. "I can't make this decision without talking to John," she told Dr. Stern. "Is an hour or two going to make a big difference to Roman?"

Dr. Stern shook her head. "No, I've started treatment for shock, and I won't touch him until his vital signs improve. You have a couple of hours."

Twenty minutes later Dirk followed his mother into Uncle Will's hospital room. Dad sat in a chair close to the bed, and both men looked up when they entered. When Dad stood, Mom walked into his arms.

"How's that dog?" Uncle Will asked. "I guess I owe him something even though he hit me like a railroad train."

Unable to talk, Dirk shook his head.

"He's bad," Mom said, sitting on the end of the

bed. "I need to talk to you, John." She slid off the bed and led him out the door.

Uncle Will motioned toward the chair Dad had evacuated. "Sit down, here." Dirk dropped silently into the chair. The old man watched him a moment. "Is he going to die?" he finally asked softly.

Dirk swallowed. He wanted to tell Uncle Will. In fact, he wanted to tell him plenty, but he was afraid he'd cry if he tried to talk. After swallowing several times, he choked out, "They're deciding whether to spend the money to save his life." His grief made him want to hurt the old man, but he was too emotionally drained to say anything more.

Uncle Will jerked erect in the bed at Dirk's words, then moaned and lay back. "Guess I'm going to be pretty sore," he said. Then his face brightened. "How could anyone talk about money when it comes to saving a hero's life? You get right out there and tell them I'm paying for the dog's treatment. I don't care how much it costs." After resting a minute, he motioned toward the door. "Go tell them, John."

Uncle Will didn't have to repeat his instructions. Dirk bolted through the door so quickly he missed the last words. "Roman gets to live!" he yelled. Then remembering he was in a hospital, he quieted down. "Uncle Will's going to pay," he whispered. "Let's go tell the doctor, Mom. Hurry."

Dad dropped an arm over Dirk's shoulder. "Not so fast. Mom says the doctor isn't sure he'll make it, anyway. And he'll go through a lot of pain."

"So? We know he won't live if we don't try."

"Do you think we should waste Uncle Will's money and make Roman suffer, considering it might be for nothing?"

Dirk couldn't believe that his father had suggested they refuse Uncle Will's offer to pay for Roman's treatment. "He saved Uncle Will's life!" he stormed. "He deserves to live—and Uncle Will's money wouldn't have done him much good if he'd been killed by that truck."

Dad looked solemn. "I'm just wondering if it would be kinder to Roman to put him to sleep before rather than after all that suffering."

The boy stomped back into Uncle Will's room. "Dad's not going to let us save Roman, anyway," he roared. "He doesn't care about Roman. I know he could live because I've been praying about it."

"Now, now," Uncle Will said quietly. "Open the drawer in the nightstand beside my bed and find my checkbook."

Dirk found Uncle's wallet, tie, wristwatch, and other stuff but no checkbook. "It isn't here."

"I guess I didn't have it with me. I was thinking we were on our way to the store. But I guess we weren't."

"No. We weren't."

Mom and Dad returned to the room. "I have to get back to work, Uncle Will," he said. "I'll be back after 5:00. Maybe I can take you home then." He glanced at Dirk, smiling. "And we've decided to take a chance on your hero, son. If Uncle Will was hurt that badly, we'd certainly do all we could to help him get well."

Dirk closed his eyes tightly, but the tears still squeezed through. "Thank You, Father," he whispered, "thank You for changing Dad's mind and for healing Roman too." He stopped and swallowed. "Thank You," he repeated.

"Amen!" Uncle Will said, followed by two more small amens.

"Come on," Mom said. "Let's go check on Roman."

"Come back a minute," Uncle Will called as Dirk started to follow Mom through the door. The boy returned and stood beside the bed. "I have plenty of money, and don't know what to do with it," his great uncle said. "You go for it no matter what. I'll pay for the whole thing, so don't let anyone change your mind, not even the cops. Hear?"

Dirk nodded, squeezed the wrinkled old hand, and ran from the room to catch Mom.

"He's not doing as well as I wish," Dr. Stern said when they asked about Roman. "All we can do is try."

"How much chance does he have?" Mom asked.

"He has a hundred percent chance," Dirk said. "I've been praying for him."

Dr. Stern looked surprised, then smiled at Mom. "Doesn't the Bible say something about becoming like children?"

"I'm not a child," Dirk said. "But Roman's going to live. I know he is. Somehow God told me." He turned to Mom. "And Uncle Will's going to pay. You know when he called me back? He said he has plenty of money and nothing to spend it on, and for me not to let anyone change my mind about helping Roman get well. He does have enough money, doesn't he?"

Mom shrugged, glanced at the doctor, then back to Dirk. "First off, please, please don't be too sure Roman's going to live. I can't bear to see you hurt any more than you are now. And yes, Uncle Will has enough money to pay Roman's hospital bill." She turned back to Dr. Stern. "I guess we're going for it."

The doctor smiled for the first time since they'd come in, then stood and extended her hand to both of them. "Good. Roman's too good a dog to lose if we can prevent it. Call me this evening at home." She handed the boy a business card. "In the meantime, I'll do all I can for your friend, Dirk."

No one said much at home, not even when Uncle Will arrived with Mr. Ward. Dad settled him onto the couch in the living room to read the paper and watch TV. Dirk carried the old man's supper to him and changed the channel to his favorite news before returning to the table.

"You aren't mad at Uncle Will, are you?" Mom asked when Dirk settled back down at the table.

"How can I be mad at him when he's paying?" Dirk asked. "And how can I not be mad when I remember how dumb he was? Mom, he plowed right into the road without even glancing. And I was yelling at him all the time."

Later that evening Dirk didn't get much satisfaction when he called Dr. Stern at her home. "He's pretty well put back together," she said, "and his injuries were almost exactly as I'd figured. But he isn't stabilizing as I'd like. I'm going back in a few minutes to see how he's doing. He's having all the medication he can handle. We'll be mostly playing the waiting game for a day or two," she said. "But every hour he lives we can have more hope for the next one."

Uncle Will prayed with Dirk for Roman that night, and even Mom and Dad added their prayers for the big dog's recovery, after thanking Him for protecting Uncle Will.

"But God didn't protect Uncle Will," Dirk said when they finished praying. "Roman did."

Mr. Ward smiled. "Who do you think told that dog to push Uncle Will out of the way?"

Dirk didn't answer right away. His mind recreated the accident, and he thought about it a while before he answered. "I wish you could have seen him race across the road and send Uncle Will flying," he said. "It all happened so fast I could hardly follow it."

"Flying is right," Uncle Will said. "For a second I thought the truck had hit me. I knew for sure it was all over." He was quiet a moment. "Might have been better if the dog hadn't shoved me aside."

"Don't you dare even think like that," Dad

replied. "You don't know how much you mean to me."

Dirk wasn't all that sure about it, but somehow he had faith that one day Roman would be all right.

The next morning Dr. Stern felt much better about Roman's condition. "He's trying to get up," she said. "I didn't expect that for several days."

Roman came home from the hospital eight days later, hobbling on a cast covering his back left leg, and walking as though he hurt all over. "He'll have to stay in the house," Dirk said. "The lawn isn't warm enough or soft enough for an injured dog."

Dad grinned. "It's summer you know. And tell me, where's he going to sleep in the house that's so soft and warm?"

Dirk thought a moment. "Maybe I could carry him upstairs."

"If you can't, he can sleep with me," Uncle Will offered. "We wreck victims can keep each other company."

But somehow, between Dirk and Roman's own efforts, the big dog made it upstairs. Dirk knew for sure he'd never slept better. As far as he could tell, Roman rested pretty well too.

Each day Roman reached Dirk's bedroom with less effort.

One day Dirk felt restless. Uncle Will had completely recovered, and Roman tried to pretend he was well too. "Why don't we drive the go-cart for a while?" the old man asked.

"I don't enjoy playing with that thing much anymore. Would you feel very bad if I traded it off?"

"Of course not," Uncle replied. "What could we trade it for?"

"I'm not sure, but I saw an ad in the Family Shopper for a moped. It said sell or trade. Shall I call and see if they'd like a go-cart?"

Uncle Will almost quivered with excitement as he waggled his bony finger at the phone. "Call, John. Hurry before it's gone."

So Dirk dialed the number and learned the moped owner would be interested in seeing the cart. "I'll drive the moped over there, as it's easier to get around on," the man said.

When he arrived, Uncle Will went out with Dirk to look at it. "It's a pretty color," the old man commented.

Dirk had just been thinking how terrible it looked. Almost every inch appeared dented and rust clung to each depression. But then, the go-cart didn't look exactly new either.

"Candy apple red," the man said. "Runs great too. Want to take a spin?"

Of course Dirk wanted to drive it. "I'll have to do it on the go-cart track, though. I don't have a driver's license yet."

It went all right. And after only a couple of trips around the track, Dirk fell in love with it exactly as he had with the go-cart a couple of months earlier. The man looked at the go-cart and tried it out. "Yep, that'll be just right for my daughter." He looked at Dirk again. "She's about your age and a speed maniac. I'll be back tonight with my pickup. In the meantime I'll have to ride your moped home."

Uncle Will and Dirk could hardly wait for the moped to return. "Are you really going to ride it?" Dirk asked. "You could fall off it easier than from the go-cart."

"Of course, I'm going to ride it. I've never ridden a motorcycle before."

Dirk grinned. "I hadn't either before this morning but it was simple. But it isn't really a motorcycle. More like a cross between a motorcycle and a bike."

"I'm good on a bicycle, too," Uncle Will said

proudly. "I used to do lots of tricks on them." He waved a wrinkled old hand toward the garage. "Get your wheel, and I'll show you some fancy riding, the likes of which you've never seen."

Hey, Dirk thought, *that might be a great way to get even with Uncle Will for what happened to Roman. He'd for sure take a good spill if he tried anything fancy.* But he couldn't do that. His parents counted on him to keep Uncle Will from getting injured. And to prevent him from hurting anything else as well.

Dirk shook his head. "I can't do it, Uncle Will. If you got hurt, Mom and Dad would kill me on the spot. You know how much they like you, don't you?"

The old man glowed.

"Know what today is, Uncle Will?" Dirk asked as they strolled back to the house. "It's my birthday. I've been so involved with Roman I almost forgot it was coming up. I wonder if Mom and Dad did too."

Uncle Will looked surprised. "I think they did. They didn't mention anything to me, anyway." A moment later he laughed. "You gave yourself a pretty decent birthday present. How old are you, anyway? Seventeen?"

Dirk laughed out loud. "Do I really look that old? I'm 15 today. Remember? I couldn't drive the moped on the street."

The old man nodded. "I guess I knew that, didn't I. Well, I hope Esther remembers your birthday. I notice she's getting a little forgetful, though."

Again Dirk laughed. Because his parents had always celebrated big on his birthday, he knew they wouldn't forget. "I guess the moped'll be the best present I get, even if Mom and Dad remember," he said with a feeling of excitement.

Finally Dad and Mom arrived home from work and wished Dirk a happy birthday. Dad took him aside and told him they wanted to take him out for a special dinner.

"Great!" Dirk yelled even before Dad finished explaining.

His father held up a hand. "Let me finish. Uncle Will'll have to go, too."

"Oh, Dad, I spend my whole life with him. Can't we feed him, then sneak off? Does he really have to wreck everything?"

"He won't wreck anything. He's a pretty good guy. I thought you'd have noticed by now."

"He'll say or do something dumb."

"So what? I say dumb things too." He grinned. "I believe I can remember hearing even you say something that was less than brilliant once or twice in your lifetime."

"You know what I mean."

"Well, are we all going out or staying in?"

Dirk didn't need a second to think that over. "We're staying in."

Mom didn't complain about the extra work. In about 45 minutes the family sat down to a steaming meal.

"Hey!" Dirk said after Dad offered the blessing, including asking God to especially bless Dirk through the following year. "I almost forgot to tell you, I traded off the go-cart this morning for a moped."

Uncle Will chuckled "I thought you'd never get around to telling."

"Where are you planning to ride a moped?" Mom asked.

"On the go-cart track. I know I can't ride on the road yet."

Dad chewed and swallowed before he answered. "Glad to hear it. People get hurt on those gutless wonders."

"It has a lot of power," Dirk declared. "Do you want to try it later? The man's delivering it tonight."

Mr. Ward shook his head. "No way. Those things are for kids."

Dirk met Uncle Will's faded blue eyes and raised his eyebrows. The old man smiled broadly and nodded. No one said a word. Dirk wished his father would talk the old man out of riding the moped. Even though it already looked pretty rough, Dirk didn't want it dumped. But how could Dad stop Uncle Will from riding it when he had no idea what Uncle Will had in mind. And Dirk wasn't about to become a snitch.

After they finished eating, Mom brought in several packages and laid them on the table before Dirk. He unwrapped a new swimsuit, a light blue dress shirt to wear with his new suit, and a fantastic chest of tools.

"Thanks a lot," Dirk said. "I can use those tools forever."

"We got them to help you work on your go-cart," Dad said, grinning. "The one you don't have anymore. As usual, we're a day late and a dollar short."

"I can use it on my moped. Unless it doesn't need work."

While they talked, Uncle Will reached into his pocket and placed a $50 bill on the table in front of Dirk. "Happy birthday, John," he said. "You've given an old man a lot of pleasure in your lifetime."

"Thanks a lot, Uncle Will," Dirk said, wondering

if the man was giving it to him or to Dad when he was a boy. "I appreciate that more than you know."

The sound of a pickup interrupted their conversation. Dirk rushed to the door in time to see the man drop the tailgate. As Roman bounded out to greet the man, Dirk grabbed the big dog's collar. A bunch of kids jumped from the pickup bed to the ground.

"Happy birthday!" they yelled. Then he recognized Bruce, Linden, Jerry, Celia, Roxie, and Donna. Celia strutted over to him, stood on her tiptoes, and kissed him on the cheek. Roxie followed suit. Donna looked the other way. Dirk was too surprised to get excited about Celia's kiss.

"I mentioned to Donna who I was trading with, and she insisted on bombing in on you," the man explained.

"You mean you're—"

"Yeah, I'm Donna's old man. Now, where's that go-cart? She's eager to see it."

Dirk couldn't believe his old racing buddy was getting his go-cart. He was extra glad he'd fixed it up so much. Now he wished he'd given it a coat of spray paint as well.

A few minutes later Ron loped across the road, adding his "Happy Birthday" to the rest.

With the boys' help, Mr. Kind unloaded the beat-up red moped and replaced it with the ugly rusty-green go-cart.

"You kids have a good time," he yelled, coasting down the driveway, "and get home the best way you can." He started the pickup and leaned out the window once more. "Call if you don't find a ride, Donna," he bellowed.

"We came to see your first ride on the moped," Ron announced, "and wish you a happy birthday, of course."

"Yeah, hit the road," Bruce called.

"No can do," Dirk answered. "This is only my fifteenth birthday."

Just then Uncle Will came out to join the kids. Dirk felt like yelling for him to turn around and go back into the house. Uncle Will was the reason his friends hadn't been over for several months.

"Have you ridden it yet, John?" Uncle Will asked.

"Not since this morning," Dirk replied. "And I'm not John!" He almost felt guilty for shouting at the old man, but why did he have to be out here, anyway?

After Dirk made a few laps around the track on the moped, he let all the other kids have a turn too. Roman trotted behind Dirk when he rode, but stood beside him when the rest rode on it.

"How about my turn?" Uncle Will asked quietly when everyone stood around talking. The other kids, overhearing him, glanced at him in surprise.

Dirk reluctantly nodded toward the cycle. "Go ahead, take it around the track."

Uncle Will's happy smile almost made Dirk feel better, but he really wanted the man to stay out of sight when he had company.

"Help me get this thing started," Uncle Will said, sitting straddle the cycle as it rested on its stand.

Dirk moved to his uncle's side. "Just start pedaling real hard, and it'll start. Then I'll push you off the stand."

In a few seconds Uncle Will wobbled off around the track. "Wow!" he yelled, "this thing's more fun than the soapbox wagon." Giving it a little more speed the second time around, he gave Dirk a big thumbs up. By the third lap he traveled at a respectable speed. The young people all watched in amazement as his teetering progress gradually evolved into a smooth steady ride.

"He's pretty good, but I'm riding next," Roxie yelled. "I can't let him ride faster than I did."

"Hey, after me," Bruce protested.

"Wrong!" Jerry shouted. "I rode first before, I'm first again!"

"We'll see who's first," Linden interjected, giving Bruce a big shove. "Want to argue with that muscle?" Bruce, reeling from the blow, stumbled onto the track just as the moped roared up.

Uncle Will saw Bruce too late. Hitting the brakes, he swerved wildly to the right. After a moment of struggling, he hit the ground and slid several feet in the dust before stopping.

Dirk sprinted toward him, Donna and Ron reaching the old man at the same time. All three dropped to their knees beside Uncle Will. "Are you all right?" Dirk asked.

"Let him rest a minute," Donna said.

Uncle Will stirred and gave one soft moan. As Dirk looked at his elderly uncle's pale face, he felt his heart beat faster. What if the man was hurt badly? Uncle Will had been fantastic to him. Always. Whether he'd been Dirk or John. Whether he'd been nice to the old man or not. "Can you talk yet?" he asked quietly.

"Yes," the injured man grunted. After resting a little longer, he raised his eyes to Dirk's. "I guess— I'm—too old." He took a deep breath. After another minute, he raised himself to a sitting position. That was when Dirk knew his old great uncle would be all right.

Ron put his arms around Uncle Will and helped him to his feet. "Are you able to stand?" he asked.

"Yes, I'm all right." He brushed ineffectually at the dust on his clothes.

Donna touched his face gently. "You scraped your face and arm pretty badly, Mr. Ward. You may need to let a doctor check it over."

Uncle Will gave Dirk another thumbs up sign. "We've been hurt worse, haven't we, John? Remember the time we were hiking down to Crater Lake, and you slipped over the edge?" He laughed out loud at the memory. "I guess you thought if you latched onto me, my weight would hold you, but we sure rolled down that embankment to the next switch-back trail, didn't we?" He twisted his arm, trying to look at the abrasions. "It was worse than this. I'll live."

Ron helped the old man to the house, Donna and Dirk following behind. Celia and the others quietly drifted away. After they put Uncle Will safely in a chair in the kitchen, Donna moistened cotton balls in boiled water after it had cooled, while Mom gently swabbed out the dirt.

Uncle Will's definitely one of the good guys, Dirk thought. How could he ever have wanted to get rid of such an indomitable old man? How could he have been embarrassed by such a really good person? So what if he did get mixed up sometimes? That wasn't his fault. His big heart much more than made up for whatever trouble he caused. Then a disturbing thought came to Dirk. How could he ever live without Uncle Will to share and enjoy life with him?

Donna assisted Mom until Uncle Will's face and arm were free of dirt and sprayed with antiseptic. Ron and Dirk watched, unable to leave. Dirk knew that stuff stung, but Uncle Will didn't make a peep.

When they finished, Uncle Will raised both thumbs at Dirk. "Next time I ride that thing I'll set some kind of record," he said, grinning. Then the old man looked from Ron to Donna and back to Dirk. "You better hang onto these guys too," he said. "Genuine friends don't come along every day, you know. And you were right, John. Skin color doesn't have a thing to do with a person's character."

After a while Donna called her father to come

after her. Dirk followed her out to wait. "I'm sorry your birthday got wrecked," she said as they sat on the lawn.

His birthday wrecked? He felt as if he'd been given the biggest present of his entire life. Uncle Will. A man, who in spite of advanced age, brightened his life a whole lot. A man who knew how to live and love—and play. He should—with nearly 90 years of practice. Dirk felt fantastic. Almost good enough to fly. *Dear Father*, he said silently. *Thank you for making me keep on "doing it unto the least of these."*

Then he looked at Donna. Really looked at her, and met her caring eyes. He wondered how he could ever in all this world have thought Celia was prettier.

Also by VeraLee Wiggins

Barbie
Barbie seems to have it all until her dad's accident
changes her comfortable lifestyle. Judi and her
good-looking brother, Tom, help Barbie realize that
happiness isn't hinged on a lot of money. Paper, 128
pages. US$4.95, Cdn$6.20.

Let's Pick on Benjy!
The vicious dogs on Benjy's paper route were nothing
compared to some of the kids at his new high school.
What would it take for them to accept him? Paper, 128
pages. US$4.95, Cdn$6.20.

Runaway Love
Seriously questioning her parents' judgment, Genie
finds herself torn between keeping their trust and
losing her one chance with Paul. Do her parents just
want to ruin her fun? Or will dating Paul prove a
dreadful mistake? Paper, 110 pages. US$4.95,
Cdn$6.20.

The Bucky Stone Books

1. Making Waves at Hampton Beach High
Bucky didn't get to go to academy, so he's decided to make the best of public school, and that means sharing Christ. It's going to be a pretty radical year for everyone involved!

2. Showdown at Home Plate
It's late Friday afternoon during the championship game, and every eye is on Bucky. Should he take his turn at bat, or be true to his conviction not to play on Sabbath?

3. Outcast on the Court
Bucky has what it takes to help lead the Panthers to victory. But winning won't be easy with his fiercest opposition coming from his own coach and team.

4. Bucky's Big Break
Bucky's new job as a bank teller opens up all kinds of possibilities for his future—if he lives long enough to have one. One of his customers has a gun.

5. Bad News in Bangkok
Bucky's 9,000 miles from home, hopelessly lost on the streets of Bangkok. Somewhere in the huge city are friends he'd give anything to see again. But it will take almost a miracle to find them.

Each paperback book by David Smith is US$4.95, Cdn$6.20. Look for others in the series coming soon.